W9-BHE-664

STRYKER

by
William Crawford

PINNACLE BOOKS • NEW YORK CITY

STRYKER

Copyright © 1973 by William Crawford

All rights reserved, including the right to reproduce this
book or portions thereof in any form.

A Pinnacle Books original edition, published for the first
time anywhere.

First printing, November 1973

Printed in the United States of America

PINNACLE BOOKS, INC.
275 Madison Avenue
New York, N.Y. 10016

STRYKER

Prologue—PHOENIX PHONE CALLS

The two men waited in a motel room on Van Buren. The motel belonged to the Mafia, but a man frequently mentioned in Phoenix media for his good works fronted the operation. The larger man lay on the double bed nearest the door, slowly smoking a cigarette, staring at the ceiling, body relaxed, ankles crossed. He wore a pair of white boxer shorts.

The other man, younger and smaller, fine-boned, sat naked on the end of his bed and watched TV, paying no attention to the network newsman's words but wondering why a man who made $200,000 a year wore such an obvious hairpiece: it looked like spit-shined glossy black plastic.

The telephone rang and the younger man jumped, whipped around, staring.

Calmly, the big man swung his legs off the bed, feeling bristly carpet under his bare feet. He deliberately put out his cigarette. After the third ring, he answered, "Yes."

"It's on," said a voice the big man recognized.

"All right."

"An envelope's at the front desk."

"All right."

"Nothing's changed. It's exactly as you were told. A cinch."

"Then do it yourself, it's so easy."

"That's not—"

"Exactly. So keep your idiot opinions to yourself."

"Jeez, guy—"

The big man paid no attention. He looked at the heavy gold Rolex wristwatch with gold expansion band lying on the table beside the telephone. They had approximately forty-five minutes before the hit.

7

"Shut up," he told the caller. "Tell him his cut comes the usual way," and hung up. He looked at the younger man and nodded, and the young man grinned.

They dressed in dark, expensive silk suits, subdued shirts, carefully knotted neckties, dark socks and custom-lasted cordovan shoes. They checked the contents of their attaché cases.

While the big man stopped at the front desk and took the plain white envelope from the clerk, the younger man telephoned for a taxi. They waited inside. The sun had gone down, but the crushingly hot, humid Arizona air remained. The faces of people entering the lobby streamed sweat.

The big man directed the taxi to the nearby international airport. He opened the envelope and took out a single sheet of paper and a parking stub. On the cheap paper he read: *Black Falcon 2-door. Texas plates BWP 98.* He did not like a number so easily remembered, but the plates had undoubtedly been stolen and the car, too. Cool enough.

They got out in front of the terminal building, well-dressed businessman, expensive cases in hand, catching a flight. The young man paid, tipped a bit cheaply. They entered and walked the length of the lower floor, exited into the long-term parking lot. It was quite dark now, a bit cooler. The young man took skintight medical gloves from his case, opened the car and got in, found the key in the ashtray, inserted it in the ignition, started the car. The older man put a glove on his right hand, drove with it, bare left hand to pay at the booth; then he put on his left glove.

He drove directly back to Van Buren, turned west and followed the boulevard to Grand, turned northwest, then back east on a major cross-street until they came to a huge shopping center.

The big man turned along the west edge of the center, then up the alley, and stopped behind a chain supermarket, a few feet from the steel-plated back door. The young man handed over the leg of a pantyhose. Each man pulled a stocking leg over his head, well down over the face, flattening and distorting their noses, cheeks, features, masking

8

eye colors. From their dispatch cases each took a .357 Magnum revolver with four-inch barrel. The big man looked at his watch in the dashlight glow. "Let's go."

He set the handbrake, left the motor running and headlights on low beam. As he got out of the car, he pulled down the sunvisor, showing a stenciled card: SPECIAL DELIVERY. No cop would fall for a delivery car with out-of-state license, but the police were no factor if the finger did his job. The delivery shuck was only for curious passersby.

They walked directly to the back door and found it unlocked, according to the set-up. They entered without hesitation and moved quickly, silently, through stacked goods to the manager's office. The big man halted, then eased forward and looked with one eye past the doorfacing. The manager, of whom the big man had a photograph, sat behind his desk—slender man with bright eyes, thick moustache, and red boozer's nose. Stacks of banded currency and rolled coins lay on the desk, and the manager checked them as he punched adding machine keys.

The big man nodded and stepped soundlessly into the room. The young man followed and closed the door. The manager looked up, annoyed, then went sick with fear. In a gesture of sheer futile anxiety, he thrust his hands protectively toward the money.

"No," said the big man, with such lethal impact the manager reared back in his chair.

The big man gestured, and the younger man stepped forward, cocked his revolver, and stuck it into the manager's face. The manager's bladder let go. Quickly but methodically the big man cleaned off the desk and emptied the safe, taking silver as well as currency. It took less than ninety seconds; he used the same lock-pouch the armored car service furnished and would arrive in six minutes to pick up. The big man tossed the heavy bag across to the door, scooped the manager up, and slammed him face down on the tile floor so hard it crushed the man's nose, sheared off three teeth, and knocked him unconscious.

The young man went to the door and turned off the office light, opened the door, looked out, saw no one, moved out quickly. The big man came behind, carrying the heavy pouch easily in his right hand, revolver in his left. They opened the back door and stepped into the alley. Someone stood beside the Falcon, looking inside. The young gunman said, "Hey!"

The figure beside the car straightened up, and the young man shot. The .357 Magnum soft-nosed, cross-hatched lead bullet literally disintegrated the victim's skull, striking just above the eyebrow line, dead center. On impact the soft, split slug virtually dissolved and would be of no use ballistically.

"That was stupid," the older man said as they drove out of the alley, stocking masks removed, money pouch on the back floorboard. The young man did not answer; he only sighed deeply, shuddered, sighed again.

They drove less than a mile to a drive-in movie, watched the double feature with interest, exited with some 200 other cars well past midnight. A few minutes later they drove into the garage of a modest home, and the young man lowered the door while the big man got the money pouch and carried it into the kitchen, checked the taped-down blind over the sink, then began splitting the money. He counted out a third, using all the coin, making up the rest with bills of the largest denominations in the score. He put the silver back into the armored car company pouch, carried it out, and locked it in the Falcon's trunk. He wrapped the finger's currency in old newspaper, secured the flat packs with rubber bands, put the packets in a heavy envelope, and taped it securely. The envelope had stamps and a Phoenix post office box address already on it.

While the big man performed these chores, the younger man took the original white envelope and note, the coin wrappers and currency bands, and the stocking masks into the bathroom. He burned them carefully in a steel wastecan, then flushed the ashes.

The big man split the remaining money, all currency, exactly in half, packed each portion in a separate dispatch case. The men did not talk. They never removed the skintight rubber medical gloves. At the big man's nod the young man went to the telephone and called a taxi. A moment later, carrying their cases, they left the house, walked to the end of the block, turned south, and walked toward Indian Hill Road for two blocks, removing their gloves, discarding each singly. They climbed into the taxi and went to a fashionable bar on Van Buren not far from their motel. They had one drink and left, taking another taxi to a parking lot near the Adams Hotel, and emerged a few minutes later, luxuriating in the lavishness of their Mark IV.

While the young man packed, the big man paid out in cash at the motel, and they drove to Globe, checked into the Copper King, ordered whiskey, ice, glasses, soda, tipped the bellhop lavishly, asked how far it was to Phoenix.

The young man took one of his suitcases and rushed into the toilet. The big man shucked his coat and hung it up, stripped off his tie, turned on the TV while he mixed a dark brown drink. He sat and watched the late-late news on a Phoenix station during a break in the late-late movie.

The store manager had given a vague description of approximately three-fourths of the white American male adults in the U.S. The dead body in the alley behind the store had been named Kelly Jo Kaine, a 15-year-old Girl Scout riding her bike home from the one evening a week she spent playing checkers with an invalided old woman.

The big man felt absolutely nothing upon hearing this identification. He sipped his bitingly strong drink, lit a cigarette, continued listening to the report. The police had no statement other than the usual one that the investigation continued. One robbery squad dick admitted the score evidenced an "extremely high degree of professionalism."

When the movie started again, the big man picked up the telephone, a direct outside line not leading through the motel switchboard. He got the operator and asked for a number in Phoenix. "Hello?"

"It went down OK, better than thirty-six large."

"You call dumping a teen-age girl OK?"

"I said it went down OK, not perfect."

11

"That cowboy's going to get you nailed, shit like that."

"What's next?"

"You'd better cool it for a while."

"Bullshit! It went down OK. No witnesses, none. I mailed your package in Tempe on the way out. You know about the Falcon. I want a score."

"Christ, you've had nine in a row. You must have a hundred grand soaked."

"I don't intend doing this all my life."

"Cowboy shit like tonight and you won't need any retirement fund."

"Goddamit," the big man said thinly, "how about it?"

"You know Albuquerque?"

"Certainly."

"El Paso?"

"Are you deliberately being stupid? Maybe you're a comedian now?"

"You sound nervous."

"OK, smartass, I'll call the other guy."

"Hold on."

"Well?"

"Albuquerque, in a couple weeks, OK?"

"Sure."

"You know—"

"No names."

"The line's clean. Our guy from Ma Bell left twenty minutes ago."

"Mick Deel?"

"How did you—"

"What's the score?"

"Check into the Sundowner, and we'll be in touch."

"That's no—"

"So? You spend your own dough for a change. Enjoy. We'll be in touch. And before you come unfastened again, that word just came from The Man. He don't like that cowboy shit, that girl-killing crazy cowboy shit. He thinks the same as I do. You better get rid of that nut."

"Just tell me the score and stick the advice up your butt."

12

"You getting particular?"

"I've always been particular. I can afford to be, in case you've forgotten. My name doesn't end with an "i" or an "o" and the only fingerprint record I've got is military service. I *need* you guys like I need my balls shot off."

"Except for one thing. There wouldn't be any *you* without our organization," another voice said, a smooth, oily voice. "Be reasonable, keep your temper, and remember —though you don't have a record, we know you."

"And I know you."

Now the voice held menace, even though it remained smooth and reasonable. "But you have no organization."

The big man had for a long time been totally and utterly without fear, and he felt no threat upon his life, hearing the implication that his life could be snuffed out like switching off a light. He had known that from the moment he began sub-contracting for the oily-voiced man.

"I am prepared to offer you a better deal."

"I'm listening."

"If you'll get rid of the cowboy, for this one piece of business, I will go an eighth/seven-eights your way."

"And if I don't?"

"Can he mean so much to you?"

"If I don't?"

"You won't have to do anything. We have men to take care of such business."

"If I don't?"

The man in Phoenix sighed. "Then a fourth/three-fourths . . . after ten percent off the top for expenses, and you are on your own for personal expenses."

"That could work out less than the usual."

"Why, yes, I believe it could. But then it's your decision, isn't it?"

"What's the score?"

"Quite large. Not less than one hundred thousand."

"That sounds like a bank."

"Oh?"

"I don't do banks. You know that. They're too heavy."

"And killing children is not?"

"That couldn't be helped."

"I doubt that, I sincerely doubt that."

"I'll have to think it over."

"Yes, you do that. On your own time and money, of course. You think it over as long as you wish. . . . And I would also advise you to think very carefully about the other, too. You see, the license plates were ice cold, as was the car, as is the house. If the child had gotten a perfect description and immediately telephoned the police, we had a contingency plan. Killing her was not only stupid but unnecessary."

"All right, I'll think about it."

The reasonable voice sighed, and the extension clicked. The first voice spoke again. "He's right, you know."

"Shut up."

"Will you look it over?"

"A hundred large, really?"

"Discounting the deductions mentioned."

"All right."

"We'll be in touch. What name will you use?"

"The usual. We've got the Mark IV."

"OK . . . and you really should think about the other—"

The big man hung up and finished his drink as the young man came out of the bathroom, asking, "You're not still angry, are you, darling?"

"No," the big man said, looking at the young man, now wearing a flowered pink kimona, rouged lips, and long false eyelashes, pantyhose and spike-heeled shoes.

The big man rose, took the bottle, upended it, letting the amber heat run down his throat. He drank almost a pint without stopping, then carefully stoppered the bottle—

And fell upon the young man whom he'd indoctrinated and indentured for life.

1—FUGITIVE

Dolores Bellon stood six feet, one-half inch tall and weighed 208 pounds, a rather large girl . . . except in Spanish *dolores* means "sorrows." Any infant which caused its mother a particularly difficult and painful birth may earn the name Sorrows without being a girl-child.

None of this mattered anyway.

Except for his mother, everyone in Bellon's family and all the men he worked with called him Chino. He had slightly slanted light brown eyes and folded eyelids, which gave him an oriental appearance. His last name, also Spanish, did not rhyme with mellon; it was pronounced Bay-*yone*. He had been a cop for almost seven years.

At the moment Det/3 Bellon stood in the glare of police car headlights holding a sawed-off pump-action riot gun by the pistolgrip, gun butt resting on his hip just ahead of his belted revolver. He looked down at the dying man.

Then Bellon shifted his gaze to the man kneeling beside the fugitive Bellon had shot just seconds earlier, holding low, wiping Gomez's legs from under him as he came out the back door of the shack, shooting at Bellon.

"Nicked the femoral artery," said the kneeling man, tightening a tourniquet fashioned from the fugitive's belt. "I don't think he'll make it." The wound continued pumping blood despite the binding.

Chino squatted, holding the pumpgun across his thighs. "How about it, Spider?" Bellon asked in Spanish.

"Fok jew," Gomez panted through clenched yellowish-green teeth. "Why jew choot me, Chino? Sumbeech!"

Bellon chuckled, shaking his head. "But you popping shots at me is OK, huh? I'm a cop." Bellon spat. "You bastard."

"Ease up, partner," said the kneeling man, and Bellon

15

looked at Sgt/Det Colin Stryker again. Stryker spoke to Gustavo "Spider" Gomez: "Why don't you tell us, *Araña?* You're making that Last Trip, man."

"You send for a priest?" Gomez asked in Spanish.

"Sure," Stryker lied. "On the way. . . . Who's your *dedo,* finger, that El Paso ripoff?"

"I don' know wha-jew mean."

"You're whacked out, Spider," Chino said flatly. "Drop your mud, man. Don't be a fool. If the priest gets here for last rites you're lucky. Tell us and get it off your back."

"Fok jew, Chino! why jew choot me? Aw, *goddam!* It HURTS!" With that final scream dying out, gargling in his throat, Gomez died.

"Well, *shit!*" Stryker said, getting to his feet, an even bigger and heavier man than Bellon, six feet and three inches, 225 pounds, belly flat and hard as a bank vault's toolsteel door. He walked back to the gray Ford with bald tires and opened the door, sat down and picked up the microphone, calling central radio control.

It took hours, wrapping up the case, getting the homicide dicks out to photograph and measure and draw diagrams, taking statements, rounding up a coroner who pronounced Gomez's stiffening remains dead, ordering an autopsy, scheduling a hearing for cause of death.

As Stryker and Bellon finished their statements to the policewoman who'd accompanied Lt/Det Gunn, Stryker said, "Be goddam sure, Loot, your men find at least *one* slug from the bastard's pistol." Stryker gestured along the fenceboards. "I don't want the FBI screwing with my boy."

Gunn nodded. "I think Clint's already found one. We'll have ballistics match it up."

"Anything else? You got down just how it went?" Stryker asked the policewoman, who had folded her steno notebook and lit a cigarette.

"I have everything you said, sergeant, both of you."

"OK. Let us know about the hearing, huh?"

Gunn nodded again, absently; his attention centered on the crowd around the site—dozens, perhaps hundreds of brown faces with dark eyes. Gunn felt a ripple of fear; he always did nowadays when he came into this part of the city. He could never forget, nor did many cops—the Watts Riot started over a traffic ticket!

And no cop in *this* city had yet forgotten The Summer of '71, when outright insurrection erupted. The police station attacked. Ambulances, tow trucks, police cars and vans upset and torched. Central Avenue looking like the street of a city under attack, which it was—storefronts in shambles, buildings and autos torched, looting, rape, killing . . . warfare!

Just thinking of June, 1971, made Gunn's ulcer shoot raging pain through his guts. He took a handful of chalky pills from his pocket and began munching them like peanuts, lips whitening. He glared at Stryker and Bellon with something akin to hatred. It was all their fault. . . .

OK, so they'd *had* a warrant for Gomez's arrest. Two warrants: armed robbery and fugitive from justice. And Gunn did not doubt for a moment Gomez *had* shot four times at Bellon before Chino cut the asshole off at the knees with the pumpgun, purposely not killing when he had every right to unload high and blow Gomez's head off. But, Christ! Why in *this* neighborhood? Gunn could see brown berets on heads in the crowd, and he abruptly realized the crowd had not been silent. From it issued a solid monotone, a muttering hatred, occasionally jarred open by a long shout, run-together words in Spanish which invariably ended in a drawn-out wail.

"*Con safos,* you prick," Bellon said as one *grito* from the crowd ended, *con safos* meaning approximately, "the same to you, doubled, wrapped with barbed wire and stuffed in your ass. . . !"

Bellon parked the Ford, and they got out and went into the police station, thinking of their own reports still to be made. As they passed the open door of Burglary Squad's office, Ted Whiteclaw called out, "Hey! You took down old Spider Gomez, huh?"

Stryker and Bellon stopped. "Yeah, bled out before the ambulance arrived."

"Dumb ass," said a lean, almost emaciated black detec-

17

tive named Webster. "You get anything off'n him before?"

"Zilch."

"Never mind all that crap," said Tom Pastore, who looked more like Hollywood's typecasting of a Sicilian gangster than a cop. "Go on with it, Blanketass."

"Oh," Whiteclaw said, "well, these two buddies were camping out, see, hunting. While one guy builds the fire for supper, the other goes into the boonies for a dump. A couple minutes later, the guy at the fire hears his buddy scream like he's got a panther clawing his ass, so he grabs his rifle and takes off, finds his pard lying on the ground holding his crotch. 'What the hell's wrong?'

"'Goddam rattlesnake bit me right on the *dick!*'

"So his buddy throws him over his shoulder and runs back to camp, throws him in the jeep—they're way to hell'n gone back up in the hills, probably poaching on Reservation land—"

"Just cut the friggin social commentary, Blanketass, and get on with the story," Webster said, flicking his bony black hand.

"OK, so this dude hauls ass down the mountains to this little crossroads grocery store, filling station, post office, trading post, you know?"

"I thought you were telling a joke, *indio,* not a Rio Arriba County travelogue."

"Naw, this is important," Whiteclaw said, pushing his open palms at the listeners. Bellon looked at Stryker, who shrugged and turned down the corners of his mouth.

"It's Saturday night, see, so no one's home, all gone to a dance in Chama or Questa or some big place like that."

"I been to Saturday night dances in places like Chama," Chino said. "Good place to get your guts dumped in the dirt."

"You guys wants hear the story or not?"

"Go on, go on, so this dumbutt got his meat snakebit."

"Well, his buddy can't find no one, so he gets on the phone."

"I thought the joint was closed," Pastore said. "They bust his ass for B&E?"

18

"An *outside* phone, OK? Like a booth!"

"And he just happened to have a dime."

"Matter of fact he only had a quarter, but he dialed the operator and got it back."

"Jesus, somebody write that down," Stryker said, "a damned phone that works first time and you get your dough back. That must of been in Chimayo, where they do the miracles."

"OK, screw you white-eyes bastards," Whiteclaw said, jamming the middle finger of his right hand in the air, at the same time slapping the palm of his left hand across his right bicep. "Up yours with prickly pears wrapped in glass wool!"

"Oooooh-hoooo! That smarts, just thinking about it," Pastore said, lunging to his feet.

"Go *on,* for Christ's sake! Tell the story," Webster said. "The guy dialed the operator—"

"And got a doctor on emergency."

"Now I know it was Chimayo," Stryker said quietly to his partner, "place of miracles."

"That wouldn't be a miracle; it'd be magic."

"You guys shut up and let him tell the story."

"The doctor tells this guy, 'Well, if you got no snakebite kit, then you cut cross-hatches on the fang marks and suck out the poison.' The guy asks if that's the only way. The doc tells him absolutely. *And* he better get it *on:* the bite's close to the femoral artery so the guy could go fast. Well, he hangs up and stands there a minute, thinking, you know? Then he walks back to the jeep. His pard's already weak and sick, but he wants to know what the doc said, and the guy tells him, 'Pard, you and me been pals most our lives. I give you the shirt off my back, give you my last cigarette, let you bang my girlfriends, take my last drink of whiskey . . . but the doctor said you're going to *die!'* "

Everyone laughed.

Bellon followed Stryker down the hallway toward their office: FUGITIVE SQUAD. He said, "Before I came on the cops, I used to wonder why on *Dragnet* and *M-Squad* and such stuff they never showed cops around the station, meet-

19

ings or conferences—like that." Chino jerked his thumb over his shoulder toward Burglary. "That's why."

Stryker laughed. It was funnier than Blanketass Whiteclaw's long-winded joke. He opened the door and flipped on the light. The room stank: sweat, musty central air conditioning, tobacco smoke, disinfectant and vinyl tile wax.

They shucked their suit coats and hung them on hooks twisted into the wallboard. Stryker stepped over to the bulletin board, which covered most of one wall from three feet above the floor to seven feet up. Stryker jerked Spider Gomez's mugshot off the board, leaving a scrap under the chipped, yellow-headed thumbtack. He threw the ragged 3 by 5-inch photo (full face and left profile) on his desk, went to a bank of green filing cabinets along the end of the room behind the desks, pulled a drawer and took out Gomez's file, tossed it on the desk beside the mugshot, and said, "Dog-chowed, you asshole!"

From the side of his eye, Stryker watched Bellon: the kid had been a cop for a while, but he'd only worked Fugitive six months, and Gomez was the first asshole he'd rendered.

Some would-be athletes took a hell of a shower. Some cops got their kicks strutting around with tin on their shirts and iron strapped on their asses. But at nut-cutting time, they did not know. They thought the badge a shield—they drew iron too soon, flourishing their revolvers to put a floor under their sinking guts and hopefully intimidate men they feared; or they hooked it out and took down some innocent, spraying slugs at everything that moved. Such creeps had no business on the cops at all, but there were always some around.

Despite all the tests yet contrived, no one had yet figured any reliable way to test a man's judgment under great stress. Tests could only eliminate the obvious misfits. Those who passed underwent twelve weeks of intensive training at the academy, then a couple years OJT with senior patrolmen. The trouble with the system was, the senior patrolman might himself be a creep or a man who'd never been under the gun in twenty years on the job, so what quality of on-the-job training was that?

But Sgt. Colin Stryker did not select men because they walked slowly past his door with eager, ambitious faces.

Until tonight, Stryker had known everything there was to know about Chino available from records and background investigation.

One thing he had not known. But Stryker learned what he wanted to know when Bellon blew Spider Gomez's legs from under him after letting Spider pop four caps free, yelling at Spider, "Shuck it, asshole! Freeze or you're hamburger."

Well, prong that. Four were enough. So Chino held low and wasted Spider's legs. It was a damned shame one of the buckshot went a little high and nicked the big artery.

The hearing next morning found Gustavo Gomez's death to be justifiable homicide, committed by Detective Dolores Bellon when violently resisted during the execution of lawful orders, to wit: two valid felony warrants.

The violence of Gomez's resistance was substantiated not only by Bellon's and Stryker's testimony, but by that of Detective Clint Staggs, who matched two recovered slugs with the .38 Special Smith & Wesson revolver found beside Gomez. The gun had Gomez's fingerprints all over it, as did all six shell casings in the cylinder, the four expended and two unfired rounds.

An ugly, muttering crowd sat in brooding silence during the hearing. Uniformed deputy sheriffs and court baliffs formed an armed wall between the onlookers and the bench. When Bellon and Stryker moved toward the door, a dozen militant chicanos rose from their seats and headed for them. A squad of uniforms began forming around the detectives. Stryker shoved an elderly big-bellied deputy aside.

"The day *we* need a goddam escort is the day we turn in our badges!"

Using his loglike arms and hands the size of catchers' mitts, Stryker batted aside the first three dudes who reached him. All had long, ratty hair, headbands, leather

21

vests over naked torsos, jeans caked with grime. The biggest tried slipping past Stryker and hanging a blindside Sunday on Chino, but Bellon had no blind side. He'd served two tours with Special Forces in Vietnam as a demolitions engineer cross-trained in communications and intelligence. During the first two horrible weeks of each new recruit class at the Academy, Bellon served as instructor in physical training an unarmed hand-to-hand combat.

He downed the big dude so quickly and easily the other militants thought he'd slipped and busted his ass when Chino ducked under the looping haymaker, chopped him across the throat, and kicked his feet from under him. While the others turned their attention to the downed man, Stryker and Bellon sauntered out of the courthouse to the gray Ford.

2—MEETING

They took off their jackets before getting into the Ford. It was only 10:15 a.m., but the August sun crushed down upon the city, doubly hot to the two men after their two hours in an air-conditioned room.

As Chino drove out of the parking lot into traffic, Stryker took a pouch of shredded chewing tobacco from his back pocket, got a large pinch, rolled and kneaded it into a moist ball, then placed the chew in his mouth, back on the left side against his lower teeth. As always, he offered Chino a chew; as always, Chino refused.

"Where to?"

"Hit the freeway," Stryker said, peeling his sweaty shirt away from his massive chest, "get some wind and cool down."

"And maybe jump up an FF-Gay— Ooops! FF*Jay!*"

They shot looks at one another; then both burst out laughing. Four days earlier they had seen a hitchhiker on I-25 and pulled over. As they got out of the car, the guy saw the guns, ammo pouches, and handcuffs belted around their waists and went over the side. Bellon caught him before he hit the bottom of the concrete slope down the side of the freeway, smacked him across the back of the neck with a stinging, fiery slap, and shoved him back up toward Stryker.

The guy wore yellow elastic-sided halfboots, trousers, vest, and fingertip-length jacket, all of the same gaily patterned, flowery cloth originally intended for curtains or cheap summer frocks. Under the vest he wore a ruffled shirt. The trousers fit so tightly his genitals and the crack of his butt showed clearly. Stryker stared at him with the expression he'd long since discovered intimidated almost anyone he used it on—a mixture of absolute amazement, utter con-

23

tempt, consuming hatred, and barely suppressed anger. Webster had once described it: "No man alive won't feel like an asshole, ole Stryker sho'm that gameface of his— the way the Klan's Supreme Shithead'd look finding his old lady in a nigger ho house," he giggled, waving his bony black hands, "or yo, mother seeing you come out of the clapshack at BCMI!"

The lad in the flowered suit wilted under Stryker's stare. Head down, he mumbled, "I ain't done nothing."

"Shuck the coat, lad," Stryker said in a voice like pulling rusty nails from old boards.

The young man flipped the coat back over his shoulders and let it fall free, catching it gracefully at the center of the collar with his right hand. Stryker shot a look at Bellon, and Chino pursed his lips as though kissing, then made effeminate gestures: smoothing his close-cropped black hair, his eyebrows, with the tip of his little finger.

"Where you headed, feller?" Stryker took the coat.

"Home."

"I believe California's back the other way."

"I live in Colorado."

"Denver, huh?

"No, Creed."

"Feller, you go up t' Creed, Colorado in this rig, and I believe people might wonder about you."

"My clothes don't violate no laws." With peripheral vision Stryker saw Bellon crouched beside the AWOL bag the young man had abandoned when he ran. Bellon held up a wallet; then he held up another.

"What's your name, lad?"

"Bobby John Jankens."

Bellon shook his head: No.

"Try again."

"Huh?"

Stryker put his gameface on again, growling, "What's your name, you asshole?"

"Honest, mister, Bobby John Jankens."

Bellon's sudden voice from behind made Jankens jump outside his skin. "Then who's Frank Coldwell?"

24

"I don't know anybody by that name."

"How about Raymond Robert Redmonds? That you?"

Jankens started to turn around. "Freeze," Stryker snapped. Jankens jumped again. He swallowed, and it went down hard. Bellon rose from his crouch. "Don't run again, asshole: I'll blow you down instead of chasing you down." He tapped his holstered revolver with his right hand, then threw the AWOL bag on the hood of the gray Ford, dropped both wallets beside the bag, held two driver's licenses so Jankens could see them.

"How about it, sweet thing?"

"I don't know where those came from. What are they? You planted them in my baggage."

Stryker reached out and caught Jankens under the arms, lifted him three feet off the ground, turned and slammed Jankens' butt down on the Ford's fender. "You're thinning out my patience, asshole. Give down your milk before you give me the ass."

Jankens had stolen the wallets in a truckers' locker room in Holbrock, Arizona the night before. He had escaped from Tracy, a California penal institution often called an honor farm because Rotan, Texas authorities held indictments for him for writing worthless checks.

"You go fruity in the joint?"

"Yeah," Jankens said, looking at his feet. "I done a year in Q, San Quentin, 'fore they sent me to Tracy."

"You pitch or catch?"

"Huh?"

"Don't pretend you're *that* stupid, creep."

"What are you, a queen?"

Jankens looked at Stryker, then at Bellon, genuinely confused, then said, "I— well, I'm just reglar gay."

Stryker and Bellon burst out laughing; later, after they had booked Jankens and gone upstairs, Bellon told Webster the story while Stryker typed the report. Telling Webster was the same as broadcasting it hourly on all the city's radio and TV stations. For days afterwards, Stryker heard the refrain almost everywhere he went in the police station:

"Hey, man, you a queen?"

25

"Naw, man, I'm just *reglar* gay!"

It got old after the 500th time, till Chino brought in the new twist, running the freeways looking for "FF-Gays" instead of FFJ's, fugitives from justice.

Once the dry, hot wind evaporated Stryker's sweat, he felt stale and tired; only three hours' sleep after wrapping up at the scene, then making reports after Chino wasted Spider Gomez. Up early for the hearing. He told Bellon, "Let's get a cold one."

"That meeting still on?"

"I don't intend to kiss the son of a bitch, just talk to him."

"He'll smell it on you, and you know how he is."

"John The Baptist. Frig him. Any day I can't fake that phony out of his jock, I'll hang up my own."

In the dim coolness of The Sundowner Lounge, they got Scotch doubles in tall glasses. Stryker disposed of his chew in a napkin and dropped it in the ashtray. They nodded here's how to one another and took long swallows.

"Great stuff."

"Dandy. . . . You think he'll buy it, Col?" Bellon pronounced the diminutive of Colin Stryker's name as *Khal*, not *Coal*, as in colon, the bottom gut leading to the rectum.

"I really don't care. But, answering your question, of course he won't go for it. I already know what he'll say."

Bellon nodded. "It's an Intelligence Unit function."

"Right. And what he *won't* mention but will really mean is it might stick his ass out so someone can take aim at it."

"How the hell did such a shit make DC?"

"He takes a good exam. He's been on twenty friggin years. The civil service commission loves him, everything a cop should be: he don't smoke, drink, cuss, nothing. He wants *Andy Capp* banned from the comics. Bad influence on kids. John The Baptist Seamon, bastard."

Bellon nodded. Though he had been a detective just two years, he felt nothing but contempt for Deputy Chief of Detectives (Administration) John Calloway Seamon because Seamon was goddam *rajón*. An oversimplified translation is "untrustworthy." This did not mean Seamon was a

26

made cop, crooked, on the take. To be a *rajón* a man must have certain basic, fundamental faults and flaws; for the word comes from the Spanish verb *rajar,* meaning "to crack." Thus, a *rajón* is one who continuously manifests self-interest to the point of becoming unmanly. A *rajón* cracks and gives way and retreats and runs behind others, letting them shoulder responsibilities he would bear himself were he a man; but he is only a coward, a *rajón.*

At that moment Stryker lowered his half-finished tall Scotch from his mouth and said, *"Es muy rajado, él,"* which is as bad a thing as a man can say about another man in Spanish, much worse than such common expletives as *"Chinga tu madre. . . . Come mi verga. . . .,"* which are only nastinesses about incest and fellatio.

Once again Bellon realized how acutely he and Stryker were aware of each other's beliefs, philosophies, attitudes, attributes, and thoughts; they seemed to read each other's mind. It had been like that almost from the very first.

Almost. . . .

Getting to know Stryker took a little doing. . . .

Seamon's policewoman assistant ushered them into the DC's office after Seamon had kept them waiting fifteen minutes. He rose and shook hands affably; he was a tall, lean, craggily handsome man with a shock of bristly gray hair parted on the right and a forelock that dangled across his brow with calculated carelessness.

"Sit down, sit down," Seamon said, gesturing toward armless fiberglass chairs, the buttbreakers favored by airline terminals and bus stations.

Seamon sat down in a high-backed leather foam-cushioned chair behind his desk and picked up a folder. Stryker recognized it as the paper he and Bellon had written and he, as commander of the Fugitive Squad, had submitted via chain of command. Seamon should have read and initialed the paper and forwarded it on to his Chief for evaluation, eventual rejection, modification or possibly approval. Instead, Seamon short-stopped the paper and sent word he wanted Stryker and Bellon in for a conference.

"I've read this over, Duke," Seamon said.

Stryker felt his insides grind. He shot a look at Bellon. Bellon sat with his right hand over his mouth, hiding a grin. He knew how Stryker despised the nickname "Duke." Seamon alone on the department used it. His misguided and rather juvenile intent was to compliment Stryker.

John Wayne, who, as everyone knew, was called "Duke" by his personal friends and associates, had once portrayed a character named Sergeant John Stryker, USMC, in a picture entitled *The Sands of Iwo Jima*. Certain similarities to this character had given rise to the nickname when Stryker came on the department in the mid-'50's: he was big, strong, agile, fearless, an outstanding cop, and had himself been a Marine, a 17-year-old volunteer in the last months of the Korean War. He let it be known that he did not care for the nickname, but since Seamon thought John Wayne the absolute personification of "Americanism" and since Stryker had brought great credit upon himself and the department over the years, Seamon continued using the nickname, though all Stryker's other contemporaries had given it up almost twenty years ago. Nor had they used the nickname when Stryker returned to the department after recall to active duty with the Marine Corps in Vietnam—two tours of one year each. He was finally released as a captain, with several outstanding personal decorations, including the Navy Cross. All this impressed Seamon far more than it did Colin Stryker.

"Yes, sir," Stryker said, when Seamon did not continue, after saying he'd read the paper.

"It's excellent, of course, no question about that."

Stryker shot a look at Chino and found a stolid oriental inscrutability; then Chino cut his eyes toward John The Baptist with the look of a man ready to slip a knife between some ribs.

"Duke, it seems to me you've exceeded your brief here."

"What?" asked Stryker, as though he did not understand. He understood perfectly; he understood as well as he knew that the largest police department in New Mexico had no connection whatever with British Secret Service or Scotland Yard Special Branch, so what's this crap, coming on with lines from an English spy thriller? He put on his gameface and let Seamon squirm and then get right:

"What I mean, of course, is that what you propose in your paper isn't within your job descriptions. It's far more properly a function of our Intelligence Unit, as I see it."

"Why?" Stryker asked bluntly.

"Well, what you, ah, you're talking about here, seems to me, well, a sort of *conspiracy*, Duke, not—"

"That's true, Chief." Seamon loved being called Chief, though he was only a deputy and his duties confined to administration. He hadn't carried a gun in years. Stryker continued: "But that's only a small part of it. My main point is set out in the opening section *and* in the conclusion. We believe the research substantiates our claim—a major portion, if not all, of the truly big scores taken down in this city are set up by locals but actually committed by expert outsiders totally unknown to us."

"Well, there's what I mean, the conspiracy."

"But these men are criminals, professionals; somewhere else they are wanted, which makes them fugitives. I run the Fugitive Squad."

"Well, yes, not much argument there, I suppose."

"You suppose?" Stryker shot a look at Bellon, grimacing at the DC's obstinacy. "A man does not become an expert professional safecracker or bank robber just by deciding he'll go into business." Damned if I will call the phony clown Chief again, Stryker thought.

"That's quite so, I suppose." Seamon flashed a quick blue-white denture smile. "They serve a sort of apprenticeship, eh? Hah, hah, hah!"

"Yeah, something like that," Stryker said dully.

"Well, it's certainly an original thought," Seamon said, and Stryker felt like throwing up. About as original as a western movie . . . except for one thing: the M.O. had come into Stryker's city.

"Well, what do you think?" Stryker asked.

"As I said, very original. Of course, you realize one thing, don't you?" He smiled again, mechanically. "Your report insinuates that organized crime has infiltrated the city, that the Mafia exists and operates here."

"Does anyone seriously dispute that?" Bellon asked suddenly.

"I certainly dispute it and resent one of my own men saying such a thing."

Bellon shook his head and looked at Stryker, appealing for help. Stryker said, "Neither Chino nor I meant that there's widespread police and political corruption. Nowhere does the report say that or even hint at it. What we're digging at is very simple. It's what police work's all about—crime *prevention*."

Stryker paused, searching his mind for a way to amplify his case which he had not included in the report. Bellon said, "That assho—" Chino cleared his throat. "That Gomez we took down last night?"

Seamon nodded, as though in pain: there would be trouble over that one.

"He was involved in this kind of work."

"In what way?"

"Just as the typical case outlined in the paper. Someone in El Paso fingered the job Spider pulled, someone who lives there, who does not attract attention to himself when he's casing a place, sets everything up if he needs inside help or wants himself hit to collect the insurance and share in the loot, too. They got Gomez in to make the hit, a completely unknown outsider. The only trouble was, Spider did something stupid; he crossed the river. Since he had a narcotics conviction, he had to register. The hit went down perfectly, as slick as that one in Phoenix five, six nights ago. It was sheer blindass bad luck, like an earthquake or tornado, that the customs man who registered Spider at Cordova Bridge remembered Spider's clothing, khaki trousers, blue long-sleeved shirt, and heard a news broadcast on his car radio going home after work. He went back to the bridge and pulled Spider's file, notified the cops, who got a photo from the army and from that a halfassed make, enough for a warrant."

"But how do you know," Seamon protested, "that Gomez didn't plan the job himself?"

"Two reasons. First, he's been around. Second, he was a narc snitch till about six week ago, then quit them cold." Stryker could have added that the narcs went around and tapped on Spider a little in an effort to draw him back into line. Gomez told them to shove it, he didn't need their nickles and dimes any longer, he had his own living, an asshole who'd been on welfare 90% of the time since he'd been thrown out of the Army three years ago. He hadn't even had a trade.

Except for one thing: before his drug bust, court-martial, and bad discharge, Spider picked up a good basic knowledge of weapons. His wildly ineffective shots could be put down as a combination of fear and being stoned.

"Well, as I said, you make some excellent points." Seamon looked at a spot on the wall between the two seated detectives.

"Does that mean you'll endorse and forward it?" asked Stryker.

"Well, no, I don't believe so, at least not now. I want to study it further, take it under advisement, as the judges say, hah, hah, hah."

"Why?" Stryker demanded flatly.

"Mainly for your own good, Sergeant. I doubt seriously the Superintendent of Police would like reading this." Seamon tapped the folder cover. "You may not think so, and I accept your statement that you intended no insinuation about organized crime being entrenched here. Nevertheless, it *reads* that way. The Superintendent won't like that."

Bellon's voice crackled. "How does he like Big Sam Borchia living in the city?"

Seamon blinked and licked his lips.

"In case you don't remember," Bellon said, "Ugly Al Ruga was Big Sam's right arm, his underboss," Chino jerked his chin toward Stryker, "till the sarge blew him up at Winrock."

Seamon blinked, shaking his head. Stryker got to his feet. "Let me get this straight. . . .You refuse to pass our

31

paper on to The Man, even with a negative endorsement; is that right?"

"At this time, yes. I want to study it, and I may have some suggestions and revisions for the next draft."

"When can we expect it back from you?"

"Oh, I couldn't say exactly. Meantime, I'm sure you have plenty of work."

In the hallway going back to their office, Stryker and Bellon did not speak, each too busy silently cursing John The Baptist Seamon. They would never see the paper again. It would get lost. If they wrote another or typed a duplicate copy, that too would get lost.

"Well," Stryker said, hanging up his jacket in the office, "one thing you have to give the prick. . . .He can say no in a very nice way." He grinned.

"Beautifully," Chino agreed, his anger thinning.

They were cops, and as such were accustomed to bogging down in bureaucracy, empire building, self-promotion, competing with men in their own department and other agencies. Getting sore about Seamon's attitude was natural, but it was equally unnatural to stay angry about it, for such attitudes are the facts of a cop's life, as everpresent as making reports. They would, of course, handle this as cops always did: having applied for official anointing and been rejected, they would go ahead on their own. When they produced results in spite of Seamon, The Man would notice, commend them, and integrate the procedures into the department's regular routine. Once that happened, Seamon would without question have a slightly revised copy of the original paper typed, place his name on it as author, and pass it along with a letter claiming he'd assigned Stryker and Bellon to "experiment" with the innovation. . . .

In other words, a police department is exactly like any other organization.

Bellon's coldshot at Seamon about Big Sam Borchia had been no idle jab at John The Baptist's thin skin. In a peculiar way, Sam and his underboss, Ugly Al Ruga, had been responsible for Chino Bellon making detective. . . .

After three years and a few months in Patrol Division, Chino transferred to Selective Enforcement, a pretentious term in police argot meaning the motorcycle squad. He'd been on motors about sixteen months (and perfected his violator contact so he could almost always leave them laughing, even after hitting drivers with a $15 roller) the early summer evening he fell behind a maroon Imperial on Miles Road between I-25 and Yale Boulevard.

Part of Chino's technique included limiting or eliminating the embarrassment of drivers he stopped. Instead of rocketing up beside a car with lights flashing and siren whining, sticking the handlebar under the driver's chin and shouting, "Hit the curb, dumbutt," Clino honked a couple times and waved the driver over, no big production.

He tooted the Imperial and saw the driver look up into the rearview mirror and begin to slow the car. Then a big bulk thrust up off the rear seat, turned, looked, faced the driver, and gestured. The Imperial squatted and squirted smoky fumes in Chino's face as the driver jammed his foot down. Chino leaned left, twisted throttle, came alongside, and stuck the siren in Ruga's ear. Once more the car slowed. But as Chino watched, the man in the back seat beside a blonde with huge bosoms leaned forward and hit the driver's shoulder, and the Imperial leapt forward again.

Chino rated the Imperial, clocking it at 88 mph. At Yale Miles dead ended, and there were cars coming from both directions. When Ruga stopped, Chino parked the cycle in front of the Imperial and got off. For a moment he thought

Ruga was going to back up and drive around. He jerked the front door open. "Switch her off, pal. Get your license out!"

"Goddamit!" Big Sam shouted, "can't you see I'm inna friggin' hurry?"

Chino ignored him. "Let's see your license," he told Al again, voice hardening.

"Give the son of a bitch a sawbuck and let's go, Al. I'll break yer friggin' head, I miss my flight. . . . Wait, OK, here, copper, a goddamn C-note," Big Sam said, thrusting a $100 bill over the back of the seat.

Chino turned his head just enough, looked Big Sam straight in the eyes while he kept Al in view with peripheral vision. "I'm going to pretend I didn't hear or see that—one time. Don't try it again. I've got no business with you, so lean back, shutup, and I'll make this as quick and painless as possible."

Still staring at Sam, Chino told Al one last time, *"Your license!"*

"Look, officer," Al said, handing his license, "whyn't you let us go on up t' the airport, huh? I'll sign anything you write, up *there,* but let Mr. Borchia get there in time, OK?"

Chino took the license, walked around behind the car, and began writing, copying the license plate number. Al got out of the car and came back. "Look, pal, I'm being a friend. That's Big Sam Borchia. He wants to, he can knock your dick inna dirt. He's strong in the right places, you dig? Take the hunnert and no hard feelings."

Chino kept writing.

"You must be nuts, man! A friggin' *traffic* ticket's not worth your job! Be reasonable, fer Christ's sake."

Chino kept writing, and he kept watching. Sure enough, Big Sam couldn't stand it; he came thundering out of the Imperial. Chino had been ready. He stepped fast past Al and straight into Big Sam, who was not big at all, possibly five feet seven inches, though he weighed nearly 300 pounds. The only thing large about him was a vast, sloppy belly, not counting big behavior. Chino towered over Sam Borchia

34

and spoke distinctly. "I told you. . . . I have no business with you. . . . Get back into the car, *now!*"

"And if I don't? What then, you punk?"

"That's it, Sammy, tell the rat bastard *pig*," said the blonde, sliding over and peering out the open back door.

"Then your flight's not all you'll miss."

"You cheap punk, what is this, a friggin shakedown? You tryin' to hit me for a wad? That it? A fuckin hundred ain't enough for you? Whata ya make a week, a hundred and *fifteen*? And take home ninety? You lousy punk. . . . Al, what time is it?"

"Quarter past, Mr. Borchia."

"What time's the plane leave?"

"Twenty-seven after, boss."

Borchia reached into his right front pocket and brought out a huge roll of currency held by a thick rubber band. He slipped the band, peeled off three $100 bills and thrust them into Chino Bellon's face, and as he did so Chino grabbed the fat wrist in a viselike grip with his right hand, plucked handcuffs from the pouch on his gunbelt and locked the steel around Borchia's wrist, at the same time snatching the currency from the fat fingers and anticipating Ugly Al's reaction.

Sam, too astonished to move, stood with his mouth working like a fish out of water, but Al charged. Bellon pivoted easily, ducked under Al's haymaker punch, kicked Al's left leg from under him and clubbed him across the back of the neck with the side of a doubled fist. Al's lunge carried his head into Sam's big belly, knocking Sam down and out of breath. By the time the men regained their senses, Chino had them handcuffed, right hand to right hand. As he walked past the wide-eyed blonde, Chino said, "What did you say? *Pig?*" Chino grinned like a shark at her and let his left hand brush across his crotch. "Have a hambone, darlin'."

He radioed for a car to transport the prisoners and a tow truck. He booked Sam on attempted bribery, initialed the three bills and booked them as evidence. He booked Ugly Al on the traffic ticket, attempted bribery, assault on a police

35

officer, and interfering with a lawful arrest. He booked the girl on vagrancy.

She had 14 cents in her purse and no luggage. She gave the name Viki Barr, which sounded made-up, and Chino's belief was verified when he went up to Fugitive. Constance White had nine other aliases and a nice sheet for a 23-year-old: prostitution (five arrests, one conviction), swindling innkeeper (three arrests, no convictions, restitution made), swindling by worthless check (four arrests, no convictions, restitution made), possession of marijuana (one arrest, dismissed, lack of sufficient evidence), and a charge of forgery and passing U. S. Treasury checks, convicted, two years' probated sentence, currently a fugitive from justice on bench warrant from Federal District Court, Los Angeles, California, for violating terms of probation.

The kickbacks on Big Sam and Ugly Al, more or less what Chino expected, verified the inside dope that they were "made" guys—hooked up with the Mafia. It meant nothing to Bellon at the time. The Mafia, The Arm, The Outfit, The Syndicate, Cosa Nostra, The Organization, The Honored Society, The Office, The Family . . . or whatever name had become currently popular in media this week or day or afternoon, was a fact of life; Chino Bellon lived with it because he had to, and he had to because the citizens of his city, county, state, and nation had yet to manifest any real willingness to rid themselves of the stranglehold that organized crime, under whatever name, had upon them, morally, socially, and economically. Bellon knew organized crime existed: he saw evidences of it in his own city. The arrest of Big Sam and Ugly Al proved the organization operated there, but he did not take it seriously simply because taking it seriously, for a cop on his level (what could a motorcycle cop do about organized crime, for Christ's sake?), was a thankless, futile, and probably stupid exercise, particularly when OC assholes seemed made of rubber: bust one, sling him in the slammer, and he hit the street on bailbond before the arresting officer got his reports typed!

So Chino did not take OC seriously, and certainly not

personally, until three nights after Big Sam Borchia and Ugly Al made bond on the charges Chino filed against them.

That night Big Sam sent a couple of legbreakers around for the purpose of teaching Chino Bellon a lesson: who he'd better not fuck with, cop or not.

Chino got off at 11 p.m. and wheeled past the quick-service market near his home, a one-bedroom cottage in a racially mixed neighborhood. He tooted the Harley's horn, and the clerk looked out, grinned, and went back to the coolbox; a few minutes later he came out with a paper bag which he placed in the saddle bag Chino had opened. Chino slipped him a buck, a tip for the six-pack of Bud. They would not take his money for merchandise since the night he'd downed a stone hype spade trying to rob the place with a butcher knife long enough to row a boat with.

Chino rode home, parked the hog in the garage behind his '65 Falcon, and locked the door. He went into the kitchen and ripped open the carton, offed a cap, drank half an icy beer. He had showered and dressed in gym shorts and racers and was sitting before the TV with his third beer when the door chime bonged.

He felt his skin crawl all over, a feeling he'd learned to trust implicitly in Nam. He rose swiftly, calling out, "Just a second!" and darted to the back door, peeked and saw no one. He eased outside, thought of going back for his revolver and knew he didn't have time. He slipped along the wall to the corner, crouched and peeked around.

Two massively built men, one taller than Chino, the other shorter, but both seemingly overstuffed with muscle, stood at his screenless front door. Both men held baseball bats. The taller man stood directly in front of the door with his bat held behind his right leg. The other stood to the side in shadow, bat on his right shoulder like a guy stepping into the box for his swipes.

Chino grinned like a shark and backed away from the corner of the house. He took off his racers and in sock feet went around behind his house and opened the box where the yardboy who came every other week kept his tools.

37

Chino took out the rake and hefted it. It had a handle about five feet long. The head weighed about three and a half pounds and was about two feet wide, the tines four inches long.

Chino went back to the front corner of the house, noiselessly, easy after Nam's jungles. He crept around the corner in a crouch. The tallest man jerked the chime lever again calling out, "Hey! Bay-*yone!* Hustle it up! We got a letter from the Chief's Office."

Chino crept in range. He raised up, rake over his shoulder. "What's the message, boys?"

He swung as he spoke.

The rake struck the man with the bat on his shoulder under his upraised right arm, the impact driving the tines in, splintering ribs, puncturing flesh, drawing a girl-like screech from the man.

As the rake hit the man, followed instantly by pain he could not believe, he humped and jerked and doubled, his bat flying high.

Chino moved in, leaving the rake tines embedded in the man's side, and he caught the flung ballbat by the barrel. He used it like a lance, or more properly like a riot control baton.

He jabbed the small end of the bat into the tall legbreaker's side, and he grunted hard, clamping his arm down over the hurt, and at the same time unwound with the bat in his right hand. Chino ducked under the wild swing, thrust again, lanced the small end of his bat into the tall man's throat, heard him gasp and choke down. . . .

Then, ruthlessly, Chino flipped his bat into the air, reversing the grip, and went to work. He finished, his anger drained, and then he did not know what to do with a pair of shitheel legbreakers obviously hired by Sam Borchia lying on his doorstep, neither of which would go anywhere soon: both had bags of bonechips where their kneecaps had been, and the short asshole breathed blood bubbles from a punctured lung.

Chino knew he'd get a civil rights beef if he called in and had the cops—his fellow officers—come out and take the

38

legbreakers into custody. His own department was no different from any other. There were always a few ruthlessly ambitious sons of bitches who thought snitching off on other cops a sure route to promotion; and, of course, there was always the FBI.

Chino went back inside, dressed, armed himself, scouted the neighborhood, and found the legbreakers' car and driver hiding in the carport of a vacant house two blocks down the street. He crept up beside the car door, placed the icy muzzle of his .357 Magnum Colt's Python in the man's ear, and cocked the revolver. "Move and die, asshole." A rotten stench gushed up from inside as the man's bowels failed him.

Chino got the driver out, dropped him with a short up-chopping left hook under the heart, and dumped the unconscious man onto the back floorboard. He downed all the windows and turned on the air to blow out the stench. He drove back and loaded the legbreakers into the car, then picked up a partly used five-pound bag of sugar, an icepick, a butcher knife, and an eighteen-inch steel wrecking bar. He drove the virtually new (2709 miles on the odometer) Mercury hardtop toward the exclusive price-restricted-estates neighborhood where Big Sam lived. As he drove, Chino devastated the Merc's interior with the butcher knife, slashing the red leather seat covers, the white headliner, the cut-pile carpeting. With the wrecking bar he ripped the dashboard apart and smashed the AM-FM radio and tape deck. He pushed the electric buttons and raised the windows, smashed them out with the steel bar, then lowered them again as far as they would go.

He found the street on which Sam lived, coasted to a stop about a quarter of a mile from Sam's house, cut the lights, put the car in park, and got out. He poured the sugar into the gas tank. He icepicked the tires. He smashed the rear window, the tail lights, the headlights, the front window with the wrecking bar. The tires had gone flat by the time he climbed back under the wheel. The engine started lugging down.

Chino drove with his head out the window so he could

see. He drove the car right up into Sam's long, curving driveway, engine sputtering, flat tires cut through so the steel wheels grated and crunched on the white gravel. He set the hand brake, got out, left the seizing-up engine running, took one of the ballbats and wedged it between the seat and the horn ring, then ducked into the shadows and ran as the horn blew raucously and without letup.

Chino loped steadily along the wide, curving street as lights began coming on in Sam's house and the houses on each side and across the street.

The next day when Chino reported to the motorcycle squadroom, he had a message, a telephone number. He called after the squad meeting.

"Yeah," answered a growling voice.

"This's Chino Bellon."

"Get this, you fucking greaser! Lay down and quit breathing," the growling voice said with menacing hatred. "You're already dead."

Chino laughed and heared the other voice gasp. Then Chino said, "*You* listen, you friggin ghinny asshole. Where the hell do you think you are? New York, Jersey, Province, that shithole called Chicago? This ain't a *made* town, you stupid shitheel. I'm not a *made* cop. This ain't a *made* department. You're damned lucky you got them back alive. You won't again. Send more, and before they whack out, I'll have it on paper with names. I learned some stuff in Southeast Asia that'll crack a certain fat ghinny in ten seconds flat, like a cattleprod so far up your ass you'll taste the handle."

"Big talk."

"Try me, you lousy bastard. But before you do, check around. Find out what I did for a living before I came on the cops."

"Yeah?"

"A demolitions engineer in Special Forces, that's what. I can bring that big fancy pad of yours down around your ears, Sam, and not crack a pane of glass next door. You wanta go to war with me, asshole, you're gonna lose."

Chino hung up. He never heard from Sam again. Sam

40

never bothered him again. But for a long time, Chino never went unarmed; he stopped bringing visitors home; he put out a word privately to the patrol crews working the district where his mother lived, and every time he went home, he went as though entering a mine field.

Then one day about three months later Chino spotted Ugly Al Ruga in an old Chevy at Winrock Center. Al had on wraparound sunshades and a low-pulled cap. He sat under the wheel, car motor running, in gear, brake lights glowing.

Chino parked his Harley behind a Volks minibus covered with handpainted flowers and pleas for love and peace and called for assistance.

In less than a minute a gray Ford with bald tires crept to a stop behind Chino, and a huge man who certainly belonged in the NFL got out. "What's up?"

"Who're you?"

"Stryker, Fugitive Squad, what've you got?"

"Know him?" Bellon crouched and looked through a car's windows pointing.

"Ugly Al Ruga, at least that's what he calls himself around here. Works for Sam Borchia." Stryker glanced at the motorcycle officer's nameplate above the uniform shirt's right pocket flap. "Bellon. . . . Ah, you had a *barulla* with them, couple, three months ago, right?"

Chino nodded.

Stryker grinned. "I liked how you handled those pukes Sam sent after you."

"Wha—?"

Stryker grinned like a starved wolf. "Would you really have blown Sam up if he came after you again? Or sent someone around your momma's place?"

"You're friggin' A-well right I would have," Chino said flatly, looking into the greenish tinged brown eyes in the deeply tanned face. The quick grin came again, wolfish, mean, and there seemed to be a flashing spark of fire deep in the eyes which looked at Chino, unblinking.

"How did you know?"

41

The left corner of Stryker's mouth twitched, but it has the effect of his shrugging his shoulders. "Certain phone numbers, an officer gets a message to call them, we monitor."

"Who is *we?*"

"What do you think you've got here?"

Chino reached down and deliberately unsnapped the safety strap on his holster and placed his hand on the butt of his revolver. "Let's see some credentials, Stryker."

For a moment their gazes locked: then Stryker's mouth twitched again. "My inside jacket pocket."

Chino fished out the case and opened it, saw the gold Sergeant Detective badge, the ID card with a color photo of the big man standing before him.

Chino handed the case back. "I think Al's a wheelman. He's pulling something. Some other guys are in there, somewhere," he jerked his chin at the vast shopping center with its bank, jewelry stores, loan companies, supermarkets, superpharmacies, furriers, exclusive shops.

"It doesn't figure, but I think you're right."

Without another word Stryker moved back to the Ford and unlocked the trunk, took out a sawed-off pump-action riotgun, loaded it, took off his suit jacket, and pinned his badge to his shirt. He strapped on a wide belt filled with 12-gauge 00-buckshot shells.

Bellon could not believe the size of the man. With his coat off he looked twice as large as before. Arms like logs covered with reddish fur emerged from short sleeves. The shotgun looked like a toy replica in hands the size of first-base mitts. His hair, close-cropped, graying at the temples, had started thinning on top. Bellon estimated Stryker's age at forty, give or take a couple years; yet the big man's belly had no sag, and he moved like what he most resembled: the NFL coaches' dream—a huge, quick, powerful, fearless, white running back. Stryker had the moves, lithe body control, springy step, alertness, economy, and fitness: he positively exuded an atmosphere of barely controlled, suppressed violence . . . or more properly, Bellon amended

42

his thoughts, an eagerness and anticipation for impending violence.

Having been a Green Beret some four years, more than two of them in combat, Chino Bellon knew and recognized the type. He had seen several boss stud hosses in his time, dudes actually addicted to danger; he candidly admitted, in rare moments of introspection, that he possessed more than a trace of the qualities himself. He'd felt no sorrow, no pity, no remorse, and no sense of wrongdoing whatever the night he scragged Borchia's legbreakers and destroyed the car; and he'd told Stryker the truth: if Sam had monkeyed with him again, or with Chino's mother, Chino would have taken Sam's house down, family, visitors, hired help and all, and not looked back. It was still all one and the same to him, the decision he'd made while in Academy. The cops had not hired him to get hurt or maimed or killed, and if he allowed himself to be, without doing *every*thing and *any*thing he could to avoid it, including killing, he'd be personally guilty of unforgivable stupidity and totally responsible for his own injuries or death. No friggin way. . . .

Another plain Ford arrived and then a black and white, and Stryker positioned the men, assuming instant command with a presence and authority Bellon had not witnessed since his release from military service, and there only rarely.

There were four of them when they came, later identified as Tuerto (One-eyed) Casas, Billie Darness, Billie's twin brother Willie, and Sal Brazzi. They wore ski masks, long-sleeved shirts, cotton gloves with "gripper" palms, and each man was armed with a handgun. They'd ripped off a savings and loan and the jewelry store next door on the central mall of the shopping center.

When they came, Stryker gave the signal, a shout, and stepped from concealment facing the Chevy with Ugly Al behind the wheel; and a dozen other cops seemed to rise from the earth, drop from the sky, emerge from the brickwork. Al panicked. He released the brake and stomped on the gas, bearing down on Stryker.

43

Stryker stood with the butt of the pumpgun resting on his left hip. He shouted massively, must have been heard in Santa Fé. He held up his right hand, open, palm toward Al, like a goddam traffic cop. "STOP, AL! STOP! WE'RE COPS!"

Al hunched forward over the wheel, foot to floor.

Stryker shook his head. Bellon remembered it afterwards as something almost akin to sorrowful resignation. The car never wavered. It closed on Stryker, increasing speed fast. Bellon tried to cry out warning, found his throat closed. And then, almost as though he watched a Peckinpah movie's slowmotion sequences, he saw Stryker whip the shotgun to his left shoulder and fire, pump and fire, pump and fire.

The first load of buckshot shredded the right front tire. The second load went through the grill. Al fought the wheel and kept the car headed toward Stryker.

The third load unfaced Al.

The wheel slipped from his lifeless hands, the violent pull of the destroyed right front tire jerked the Chevy into a parked green Plymouth Fury III; then it sheared off and splatted head-on into a three by three by four-foot concrete block supporting an embedded forty-foot tall light pole. The pole swayed, and two bars of mercury vapor lamp fell free and landed, shattering, on the Chevy's roof.

Only Tuerto Casas tried to go for it, and Patrolman Pete Beech put three in the 10-ring (Tuerto's chest) after taking one through the right thigh.

The Darness brothers and Sal Brazzi threw their guns and the loot bags and shouted "DON'T SHOOT, DON'T SHOOT, I GIVE UP, I GIVE UP, DON'T SHOOOOOOT!"

Bellon followed Stryker to the wrecked Chevy. As Stryker reloaded the shotgun, feeding shells up the underside loading slot, apparently without consciously thinking of his actions, Bellon watched him closely.

Once more Stryker gave that almost sorrowful head shake, then he stopped beside the car and looked into the open window. Ugly Al could no longer be considered ugly. He no longer had a face at all. The full load of 00-buckshot had hit him in the face, carrying along with it splinters of glass, rubber, and metal from the windshield wipers, plastic bits of steering wheel, all embedding in the bloody pulp.

Stryker worked his mouth, turned his head and spat a thin brown stream of tobacco juice. Bellon knew then Stryker had a chew in his mouth, not a slightly disfigured jaw from some past injury, as Bellon had first thought. "Old pumpgun holds a hell of a pattern, huh?"

Bellon shot a look at Stryker. No, he was not smiling.

Again Stryker spat and shook his head, then spoke: "Damn you, Al . . . you asshole! Why'd you make me kill you?"

After a moment, Stryker turned to Bellon and spoke in a wooden voice, face impassive, "Get on the horn and call out the homicide dicks, the crime lab unit, ask for more uniforms to control this crowd, and tell control we need a coroner. . . ."

Hours later, when the investigation finally wrapped up, Stryker found Bellon. "You busy in the morning?"

"No, sir."

Stryker's mouth twitched.

Bellon said, "OK if I ask you something?"

Stryker nodded.

Big sumbitch ain't much for small talk, thought Bellon, then asked, "How'd you get here so soon?"

"I just came from the bank."

Conducting any kind of personal business while on duty was absolutely prohibited by the *Departmental Rules, Practices, and Procedures (Amended)*.

Bellon grinned, but Stryker gave away nothing, his dark face expressionless, sharing no little secrets of chickenshit rulebook violations.

Bellon could not judge from his face whether Stryker was as dark as he seemed, or if this impression came from from the contrast with his light greenish brown eyes; or if the eyes seemed paler than they actually were because of the skin's darkness.

Stryker said, "That was good work, Bellon. A good eye,

spotting the late unlamented Ugly Al Ruga. You'll get a letter."

Bellon shrugged. "I had plenty of help, thanks to you taking over."

Stryker's mouth twitched. Bellon couldn't tell if the big bastard meant a smile or sneer or had a nervous tic. "What did you mean? When you said it didn't figure, Al wheelman for a daylight hit?"

"Come by the office in the morning, and we'll talk about it." Stryker worked his jaw and spat a long thin stream of tobacco juice. "Ten, ten-thirty, suit you?"

"Whatever you say."

"See you then." Stryker walked to his car, got in and drove away.

Following a two-hour interview and lunch next day, Stryker arranged for Bellon's transfer. They had worked as partners since that day.

4—FINGER

With unconcealed disgust, Harmon Robey looked across the table at Sam Borchia. Robey flicked a glance toward the fine-boned young man to his left; he saw astonishment on Stephen Ray's face as he too watched Sam stuff food into his mouth with both hands, sauce running down his fat, dark chin.

"Come on, you guys, what-sa matter, you don't like Bella Napoli chow? This the best authentic you gonna find in *this* town!" He swept up his wineglass and slurped noisily, then belched.

Robey snatched up his napkin, wiped his mouth, rose and threw the napkin on the table.

"Hey!" Sam said, eyes popped wide, staring up at the big man, "what-sa matter with you?"

"Eating with you is like shoving for a place at a hog trough," Robey said. "You're making me sick."

"Well just screw you and the horse you rode to town on," Sam said, not convincingly. He'd felt unsure since Ugly Al Ruga got blown up. For an instant, Sam tasted the bitterness of hatred, thinking of Bellon . . . and Stryker, which ran chills up Borchia's spine. He'd arranged a talk with Sal Brazzi after Stryker rendered Ugly Al, before Sal went up to Santa Fé, the state pen; and Sal described how that goddam man-mountain stood like a bridge pillar shouting at Al, give it up, and then . . . Jeez-uss!

Something had to be done about that pair, Stryker and Bellon, Al decided, after his talk with Sal. But who the hell could handle it? The Nationals, Sam knew, would not even consider sending a hit man on contract for two cops. They'd think Sam had gone insane if he asked and hit him to protect themselves. Sam had it for himself, but with Al

47

gone and his legbreakers crippled, Sam had no one with enough balls for the job.

Until now.

OK, these guys had a thing, a pair of fruiters, so what! The old joke, some dude tried rolling a queer and got his head caved in—"Two things I love doing, sucking and fighting."

The guy in Phoenix had warned Sam, and even after he knew they'd arrived Sam put off calling them; fruiters made his skin crawl. Then he got the whole story, not just the Phoenix job when the young guy, the crazy, hit the kid in the head, but on eight other jobs this pair had pulled. They could do it, and Sam would make it worth their while . . . and he could stand personal abuse; his mentor taught him that. . . . Joe Bananas: grin and smile, pat'm on the back and buddy the bastards, fifteen years if that's what it took, then wipe it clean with one stroke.

That's exactly what Sam intended doing. Finger the rip-off and $20,000 bonus for icing Stryker and Bellon, take the fruits to the mattress—then blow them up. . . . Sapper could do that, easy.

Nobody, no son of a bitch ever lived or could be born, treated Big Sam Borchia the way Bellon had when he arrested Sam and later on the phone, how Bellon talked . . . what had he said?—

"You make war with me, asshole, you're gonna lose!"

I'll show him who's asshole, Sam thought; but in my own good time and a place I choose! The same with this snotty big bastard. Hog at the trough! Son-of-a-bitching queer!

Sam grinned, and said, "OK, Robey, scuse-a me, huh? And my peasant manners. I only own the place, but scuse-a me, OK?"

Robey turned toward the toilet. Sam smiled at the younger man. "So your name's Steve, huh? Unless you don't like familiarity and want I should call you Stephen. Or Mr. Ray?"

"Steve's fine, Mr. Borchia."

"You're a nice boy. You ever want out of this biness, you're in, come see me. I got work for you. I pay good,

Steve, you understand? Grand a week, make it fifteen hundred, and I give you a living, nice easy action, all you do is make collections, gross a hundred grand a year! But I put you down on my packing company payroll, keep OK with the income tax. You like that?"

Sam found this talk an effort, as though he were some old Brooklyn greaseball. Actually, Sam had never even *seen* a real old Moustache Pete; his accent and phraseology and mannerisms for this shuck came from movies and TV!

"Sounds great, Mr. Borchia," Steve answered.

"Call me Sam, kid! We're all friends here, even if I slopped around and offend your pal."

"Don't mind Harmon, Mr. Borchia—Sam. He's rather, well . . . fastidious."

"It's OK, OK, Steve, no sweat, I don't take offense so easy." Sam made himself laugh. "My wife tells me the same thing, for Christ's sake." His wife tried it once years ago and Sam knocked her across the room, costing him $1100 for dental bridgework replacing three upper and two lower teeth.

"I'm just saying there's more you guys can make here than what you think."

"How's that, Sam?"

"I want a couple guys hit."

"Don't you have headcrushers in your Family?"

"First, I got no Family, kid. Knock that off right now, OK? I'm an independent binessman, this place, some construction and real estate interests, a piece of an escort service, meat packer. I came up the hard way, kid, no education, no favors, no nothing, and I made it, you know, like the American dream?"

"What's the pay?" Robey asked from behind Sam in a deadly voice.

Sam's bulk kept him from moving fast or turning around in his chair. He tipped his head back so he caught a glimpse of Robey.

The questions impressed Sam: "What's the pay?" Not caring who they hit.

"I told the kid . . . I can put you on steady, fifteen

49

hundred a week each and your own living." Sam shrugged. "You don't like that, ten grand for the hits, two guys."

"We'll take the hits," Robey said.

"Whatever you say."

"Exactly."

"It's heavy," Sam said, getting a kink in his neck. He gestured, and Robey resumed his seat across the table from Sam.

"Family people?" asked Robey.

"No."

"Then it's cops."

Sam nodded and took a gulp of wine. He wiped his lips. "I'll tell you now, these aren't just *any* cops; they're a pair of bad sumbitches."

Robey snorted and the kid, Ray, smiled contemptuously.

"OK, if that's how you want it; but I want the job *done,* dead-bang!" Sam clapped his palms together with a meaty smack. The kid grinned wider, and the big guy sneered openly.

Sam shook his head. "I think I'd better tell you something about *these* cops. Just might wipe the wiseass looks off your goddam faces."

Sam told them how Chino handled the legbreakers Sam sent after him and what Chino did to the new Merc. He told them about Stryker, not only how he'd stood in there with Al Ruga bearing down on him before he blew Al up, but *all* about Stryker, his war record and his police career.

The fruits stopped grinning, Sam noticed with satisfaction, when he stopped talking and wet his mouth with another big gulp of wine, draining the glass.

"You thought I's some kind of big'n easy, huh? Offering ten grand to hit a couple hick cops in the head? What-a you think now, boys?"

"We'll take the job," Robey said slowly, "but it'll take some time."

Sam nodded, grinning himself now, meanly.

"You want them down before or after the other?"

"No time before. That's set for Friday night."

"Makes it rough."

"Also expensive—for me. I got some action around, but don't pluck ten grand off bushes!"

"Will we be hot after the score?"

"No way, man. Are you hot in Phoenix? Even after whacking out that kid?"

"Shut up about that," Robey said. "I've heard all that I want to hear."

For a moment Sam said nothing, then he leaned forward and stared at Robey. "Gunner, let me put a buzz in your little ear. Without me, you've got exactly zero. Without *us,* even less, because you can *lose* all you've soaked. I let you talk to me like I's some kind of shitheel ghinny clown a while ago because it suited me, was to my advantage. No longer."

Sam reached up and pulled his tucked napkin from his collar, balled it in his fat fist. "All I do is pitch this," he jiggled his hand up and down, "and you guys get shotgunned right where you sit. You don't believe me, look over my shoulder."

Robey had noticed the two men in wheel chairs when they came into the restaurant's private dining room but had given them no more than a glance as they expertly maneuvered their electric motor-driven chairs to table, ordered, began drinking and eating. Now Robey saw the two men had backed away from the table and sat facing him with blankets across their laps and wrapped around their lower legs. Borchia made a gesture and both men flipped back a corner of their blankets, revealing the black deadly holes of sawed-off shotgun muzzles.

"How about it, gunner?"

Robey shrugged. He knew he could live, but he'd most certainly lose Steve. He made Borchia wait, then nodded, and said, "OK."

"You got it straight? Absolutely straight? I'm a man of respect! That's how you treat me!"

Robey nodded.

"You don't seem very convinced."

"What should I do, kiss your butt?"

"It's an idea. . . . But right now I'll settle for you wiping that wiseass look off your face, gunner. That's all you *are,* remember? A goddam gunner, coldblooded bastard killer, who don't even set up his own jobs, but takes, takes, takes because you got a ton of balls and no friggin brains. That's the life you want, fine with me. But, gunner, don't forget your goddam place again, huh? You're *hired* help! . . . Now, you gonna try us or what?"

Robey lifted his left hand in a gesture that amplified his words: "OK, I shot my mouth off. . . . Sorry."

Sam's good humor returned instantly, and he carefully put the napkin down on the table in front of him. The men in wheelchairs, the legbreakers Chino Bellon crippled for life, flipped their blankets back over their shotguns, but they did not move or take their watchful gazes from Robey and Ray.

"How about some coffee, you guys? With brandy and a real Havana to polish off the meal?"

"Sure," Robey said.

"Just coffee for me, Mr. Borchia," Stephen Ray said. "I don't smoke or drink."

"Good for you, kid. And call me Sam, huh? Keep those good habits and you'll never get like me, a slob!" Sam laughed and patted his bulging belly. "I got twenty, thirty grand invested in this, over the years." He laughed again. . . .

But Robey noticed Sam's cold, reptilian brown eyes never joined in the smile, nor did the watchful men in wheelchairs flanking the table. Robey said, "OK if we talk now?"

"When you guys're ready."

A waiter, summoned by some signal neither Robey nor Steve noticed, suddenly appeared beside the table with a small cart on wheels. The trolley held a thermos jug of coffee, cream and sugar, various brandies, a humidor of authentic Havanas, recently smuggled across the Mexican border west of El Paso. They took coffee, Sam and Robey lit cigars, and Sam poured brandy. Then Sam Borchia fingered the score:

"It's a bank. We'll go look later on. You guys know the city at all?"

52

Ray shook his head: No. The big man said, "I've been in and out over the years. Back in the fifties I knew it real well; but it's doubled in size since then, maybe more. We'll have to give it a good checkout."

"We can't postpone the hit," Sam said.

"I didn't say that," Robey snapped, then made himself smile. "This is Tuesday. We have all day tomorrow, Thursday, and Friday till it goes down. No sweat."

"So what do you need?"

"An ice cold inconspicuous car that's completely reliable."

"What else?"

"The drop. A residence with a garage is best."

"I can work that out."

"Tomorrow?"

"Sure. There's vacant houses—"

"That's stupid. We want an *occupied* home, with the people gone all night. Better if they go for a long weekend, Friday through late Sunday—*But!* They don't tell anyone, like a neighbor who calls the cops when we drive into the garage. That's why a vacant house is no good, see?"

"Sure, that makes sense."

"Can you handle it?"

"I'll send one of the boys," Sam jerked his chin, indicating the men in wheelchairs, "out of town with his family. I got some biness in Raton needs looking at."

"That's it, then."

"You sure?"

"Shouldn't I be?"

"That's what I'm asking."

"Then ask straight, for Christ's sake!"

"Him," Sam said, jerking his pudgy thumb at Stephen Ray. Sam saw instant anger flash into Robey's blue eyes, and Robey said, "What we do—"

"Just shut up, gunner!" Sam leaned forward, spoke with a grinding voice: "Get this. I could not give a shit less what you creeps do with one another, to anybody or any*thing*. Go fuck wildcats or jackoff a hydrophoby skunk for all I care!"

53

Sam jabbed the hot end of his cigar at Ray. "Have you still got the gun you took that kid down with in Phoenix?"

Steve nodded.

Sam put his cigar down and held out his hand.

Ray looked at Robey. Robey looked past Sam at the two cripples and found himself facing the shotguns again. He looked at Steve and nodded. With extreme care, Ray opened his coat, reached around to the small of his back, with two fingers drew the revolver and slipped it under the napkin on his lap. "What have I got?"

"S & W Combat Masterpiece, .357 Mag. Accurized, like polished silk inside, all the moving parts." Ray nodded towards the big man. "Harmon knows weapons; he did the work."

"You understand why I'm taking it?"

"We understand why you think you *should* take it," Harmon Robey said, "but it's not necessary."

"You think nothing ever goes wrong, huh?"

"Anything can go wrong. The sons of bitches running the country may blow us all up with their goddamn bombs before midnight. But the gun's OK, Borchia. First, I make a special ammo. It disintegrates itself on impact. No ballistics man in the world can match a slug to that gun unless he fired the rounds himself into a watertank. Besides that, to make absolutely sure, I worked the gun over in the motel room, while we pissed away a couple hundred bucks apiece of our own dough waiting for your call."

"None of that crap," Sam said. "The Man gave you plain and fair warning. You don't like paying your own expenses, do what The Man suggested."

"What's all this?" asked Steve Ray.

"Never mind," Robey said quickly. "It doesn't concern you, Steve."

"Like hell," Sam growled.

"What is it, Harmon?"

"I said never *mind,* Steve!"

Ray bowed his head and clasped his fine-boned hands in his lap. With disgust, Sam thought, Jesus, he even acts like a cunt. . . . But some mean bitch, way he blew that girl's head off. . . . Christ!

"How about it?" Robey asked. "The gun."

"OK," Sam said, handing it back, realizing he had no control over the situation regardless of what he did. Robey may or may not have worked it over; this may or may not be the gun; nothing kept them from switching guns. The main thing was that special ammo. He got that straight from The Man. The slug so devastated Kelly Jo Kaine's head the morticians could do nothing, and she went in a closed coffin. The cops and doctors found nothing but tiny lead slivers.

"Let's go take a look," Robey said and got to his feet. He took out a moneyclip, peeled $10 off his wad and dropped it on the table, turned toward the door with Steve right behind him.

An hour later, they drove back toward Bella Napoli. Sam said, "What-a ya think?"

"It's a cinch."

"I knew you'd like it. How you gonna take it down?"

"Our way. All you need do now is provide the car, the drop, your envelope with postage and an address on it, fake out the cops. We'll take care of everything else."

"Oh, sure!" Sam said. "Big deal. I've been working this out for better'n two years. You'll take care of everything! You been blowing smoke up your own asses and reading your press clips. There wouldn't be a ripoff if I hadn't worked my ass off setting it up. What's you think? I drove past one day last week and told myself, now there's a place looks easy to knock over, huh?"

"OK, OK, you're a big planner; you also get a big hunk."

"I also made the asshole inside who unlocks the door and switches off the alarm. I've got ten grand invested in him."

"You may have him on the hook for ten G's, shylocking," Robey said, "and getting five hundred percent plus vigorish a week off him; but you're on the hook for nothing."

"If you don't count my time."

"I don't. It's your time, and you chose this way of using it, I didn't."

"OK, but you're sure you're straight on it? Just how it goes down?"

"We've got it. What about the car?"

"I'll call you."

"Give us a number. We'll be out most of the time between now and Friday afternoon, checking routes and all."

"OK, write this down," Sam said and gave them a number. "I'll have someone on round the clock, so call any time."

"No rental car, and nothing stolen locally—"

"Robey, how old 're you?"

"Huh?—Thirty-five, why?"

"I'm fifty. I went in biness before you were born, so knock off tellin *me* what *not* to do."

"It's our asses hanging out. I'll say what I've got to say. If it bugs you, tough shit, man."

Sam dropped them at Bella Napoli and watched the Mark IV depart. Sam felt his finely tuned senses virtually shouting at him: *Cancel. Call it off*. Professional criminals know as well as do professional cops—the most unpredictable and potentially violent men and women on earth are badass mean queers, even worse than desperate stone hypes agonizing for a fix.

Sam mopped his face with a damp handkerchief as he let himself in the back door of Bella Napoli with his key. The trouble was, he could not cancel out. He needed his share of the score, which he estimated could no way be less than thirty large. The score would actually be almost twice what the gunners thought, but Sam had a fix set with his inside man. If the fruiters got tough, Sam had that fixed, too. They'd come in for $100,000 split three ways after expenses off the top. They'd settle for that, or die for getting greedy! And if they took the contract on Stryker and Bellon, Sam would never let them leave town alive.

He passed through the private dining room after looking over the kitchen where his cleanup crew still labored. He parted a curtain and used another key and went into his office. He stripped as he walked across the thick carpeting, shouting, "I'll be outta the shower in twenty minutes!"

When he emerged, wrapped in a thick terrycloth robe, she stood naked and waiting. Sam grinned as he padded heavily across the room toward her.

"What's so funny, my big lover?"

"I's just thinking what all the TV addicts'd think, if this scene flashed on the tube." Sam saw her face harden for a fraction of a second, so she looked her real age, 33, instead of the 25 she passed for in those crummy commercials and the Monday-Friday fifteen-minute bit she actually taped all at one time every Thursday afternoon, the various guests sitting around watching one another, a champagne cocktail party afterwards. It cost Sam a bundle, that kind of time and talent on a network affiliate, but she drew high ratings, and his meat packing company did better business every quarter.

If he hadn't pissed away so much dough over the tables in Vegas and San Juan and London and that lousy Monte Carlo where they'd rape a guy's blind mother. . . . Aw, screw it! Easy come, easy go. Except it never came easy. He worked twenty hours a day, holding everything together, conniving here, dealing there, running under someone another place, and protecting his own ass from the same bastards or some other bastard screwing him. He lived in a mansion, equipped with a wife who hadn't slept with him since the night that greaser cop, Bellon, dumped her ruined brand new Merc in front of the house with three cripples inside.

So, the fact was, Sam admitted, he'd keep his "TV Star" around if her ratings fell out the bottom, because she gave a pipejob like no one else in the world.

Sam shucked his robe and lay down on the bed she'd converted from the red leather couch. She knelt between his legs and placed a hand on each of her large breasts, leaned forward and worked the smooth, heavy softness around him, enveloping him in the cleft, her tongue flicking across his belly, and when he grew and grew and without realizing began muttering, she moved back, face over his groin, then lowered her head. . . .

5—ENCOUNTERS

Arnold Witterstadt held his head in his hands, sick with fear; his grinding bowels exploded again and for a moment eased his stomach cramps. He had not realized he'd started crying until salty tears ran into the corners of his mouth.

For the thousandth time, he asked himself half-aloud: "How, Oh, God! did I get myself in this mess?"

Sitting on the commode in the bank employees' toilet, Arnold found no answer because he would not allow his mind to reach back.

Arnold only knew he'd had a spastic colon and cramping guts and constant nervous diarrhea since Big Sam Borchia telephoned early Wednesday morning. "It's on for Friday," and hung up before Arnold could state the excuse he'd contrived. He had no luck at all calling Sam. At the packing plant, the escort service, the Bella Napoli . . . Sam was not in to Arnold Witterstadt. Though he knew it hopeless, Arnold left word for Sam: "Return my call, *urgent!*"

Had Arnold known how truly ordinary, actually banal, his problem was, he'd never have believed it. Nor would his guts stop seething.

Arnold Witterstadt, lately Tech/Sgt, USAF, recently retired after twenty years plus, the last fifteen an air policeman, had gotten himself into a money bind because he kept living in the semi-high style he'd grown accustomed to in service:

He had never bought food, for example; the cooks knew they'd better stay right with Arnie if they wanted to keep selling out the back door themselves. There were always nickles and dimes "confiscated" from men gambling in barracks. A weapon vanished frequently, always blamed on militant spades and spics. Everyone knew they stole weapons by the ton, arming themselves for the coming revolution. It was in all the papers! And who checked the sarge at the gate? Not his own AP's, unless they wanted a seat on the next Southeast Asia flight.

Arnold had deals on for everything, the care, feeding, sheltering, clothing, general health, and welfare of Arnold Witterstadt, free of charge.

So his entire pay and all he knocked down went for Arnold's pleasure. His appetites were considerable. He got so used to having such great fun that his commanding officer called him in and suggested Arnold put in his papers and retire—before he got court-martialed out. Arnold accepted the offer, it being one he could hardly refuse. The facts of life on the outside knocked him to his knees. His retirement pay hardly covered rent and food. He came up $500 short less than sixty days after his discharge. To his dismay, Arnold found himself peddling his stereo, color TV, Nikon camera, Philips cassette recorder, all the nice little fancy extras which distinguish the "comfortable" man from those just existing.

Unfortunately, the hockshop man Arnold dealt with also had arrangements with Big Sam Borchia: he kept Sam's money circulating, five for four per week, 25 for 20, 50 for 40, *per week.*

Naturally, the hockshop man spotted Arnold Witterstadt for a born shylocker's sucker, a four-flusher, a would-be highroller with champagne tastes and muscatel income.

The day Arnold brought in his movie camera and projector, the hockshop man said, "I don't wish to intrude myself into your personal affairs, Mr. Witterstadt, but if you don't mind my saying so . . . this is stupid. There's no reason you should give away your valued personal possessions."

"I gotta have the dough."

"But what's to accomplish? Disposing of your property? Your assets, your *capital?*"

"I gotta have the dough," Arnold repeated dully.

"May I suggest there is another way?"

"Yeah?"

"Why not borrow what you need to see you out of this bad stretch?"

"Shit! Who'd loan me money? I make application for a loan and they check me out, no way. Behind in my rent, my car's about to be repossessed——"

"I make a few loans."

"Yeah?"

"Certainly." The hockshop man waved his hand deprecatingly. "I don't ask you fill out any application. If I can help you, I will."

"I got no collateral. All I *own* is debts."

"So who asked? You want a little loan, tell me. How much you need?"

"If I told you, you'd have a runaway. . . . Like a crazy horse who dumped his rider."

"I don't think so. . . . Of course, you *do* have a job?"

"Yeah, I had to take something; couldn't make it on my retirement pay."

"And where are you employed?"

"The Bank of the Rockies; I'm Chief of Security."

The hockshop man ducked his head and made himself cough to hide the glee he felt wrinkle his face. Once under control, he faced Witterstadt, with a friendly, just-right smile. "Arnold——I call you Arnold because we're going to do business, a lot of business. Now, you can have anything you want, just tell me what you need."

Arnold borrowed $1500, but the hockshop man only gave him $1200, keeping the first week's vigorish, interest at the rate of $4 loaned for $5 repaid, per week. Arnold felt his guts sink and for a moment hesitated; then he thought about three payments behind on his car, his unpaid rent, his bookie holding $500 worth of markers who had started making ugly phone calls. . . .

Arnold took the money. Within six months he was in for eight large and shoving a ton of stuff stolen from the base through the hockshop at twenty cents on the dollar just to keep his vig paid.

The hockshop man thought about using Arnold himself, but only briefly; he knew if he did and Big Sam found out about it, Big Sam would hit him in the head; so he "sold" Arnold to Big Sam without Arnold's knowledge until the day Arnold got a phone call at the bank, some gal with a sexy, husky voice telling him he'd won an evening's entertainment at Bella Napoli. Arnold didn't question the girl. His luck had been so rotten lately he took the phone call as an omen. Everything would start sprouting $100 bills.

At the Bella Napoli, Big Sam did a job on Arnold: guest of the house, everything the very best, including the gal who phoned him, who later that night in her lavish pad blew his pipes clean, sending him out of his skull.

When Arnold got off work next day, he found Ugly Al Ruga sitting in his car in the employees' parking lot. "Sam wants to see you, Arnie."

They went to Sam's construction company, and Sam lowered the boom. At first, Arnold refused, not because he had any scruples. He'd been a thief for fifteen years. But because bank robbery was just too goddam heavy. The FBI had ignored organized crime for more than thirty years but was death on bank robbers—took bank jobs as some kind of personal insult.

Sam accepted Arnold's refusal with a smile, then tossed a couple dozen color photos on the desk. Arnold felt himself go white. He went albino when Sam tossed an envelope on the desk with the address and correct zip code for Mrs. Arnold Witterstadt, Sr., Arnie's mother. Then another envelope addressed to the President, The Bank of the Rockies, City. . . .

"OK, what do you want?"

Sam did not say; instead he asked questions, detailed questions. The interrogation lasted several hours. Then Sam told Arnold what he wanted, precisely.

After that, Arnold heard nothing. He went by the hockshop to pay his vig, and got a smile and a negative headshake. "Call Sam."

Arnie called. Sam said, "Forget it. No more vig. Call it ten G's even. We get our deal on, you're square, OK?" Then Sam hung up, and he was not in to Arnold thereafter. When Ugly Al and another gunman were killed by the police, Arnold's spirits lifted. During his meeting with Sam it had been obvious that Ruga did all Sam's dangerous jobs, or bossed them.

Then two weeks ago, Sam called and told Arnold he should come out, dine on the house at Bella Napoli. Afterwards, Arnold underwent another interrogation. Nothing had changed in the bank's operations. Sam dismissed him, and Arnold went home. A week later came the last phone call: "It's on for Friday."

Since then Arnold's seething bowels continuously threatened to betray him, and he spent so much time in the toilet other male employees began looking at him queerly, as though they suspected Arnold might be a jack-off idiot who carried porn in his wallet and whipped his meat every time he thought about it. In fact, Arnie's part in the ripoff would subject him to such intensive interrogation by the FBI he did not feel at all sure he could withstand it. As Chief of Security, he would undergo endless questioning —how the back door got unlocked and how that incredible circumstance, by some fantastic coincidence, occurred at exactly the same time the alarm malfunctioned. No way. No way, ever, at all.

Arnie's bowels ripped again, and he held his head in his hands and cried. The FBI would break him down, and he'd go to prison, unless he claimed immunity and snitched off Big Sam, in which case he'd get rendered, no matter where he went. Every day the papers had stories about guys blown up because they crossed the mob. Even inside jails snitches got murdered. No place Arnie Witterstadt could hide. . . .

He thought of biting his own gunbarrel and pulling the trigger with his thumb. He though of double-crossing the gunners, taking them down when they came in, his story to the cops that'd he found the back door unlocked and alarm switched off on his rounds, became suspicious, and just then the robbers came in, wearing masks. Then Arnold thought again about suiciding himself. He decided he would run. But when he walked into his apartment after work that evening, Arnie found Big Sam waiting.

Sam Borchia had not made a living off the foibles of mankind since his youth without becoming extremely well educated about human nature. The moment Arnie walked through the door Sam knew his timing had been absolutely perfect. Arnie had panic written all over him, as though he wore a sign around his neck: I AM A CROOK!

Without a word, Sam got off Arnie's couch, smiled, beckoned, and hit Arnie a ton square in the guts when Arnie stepped in range. Arnie shit his pants. Sam helped him to his feet and guided him to the toilet, and while Arnie showered Sam spoke. When Sam left, he knew Arnie had shucked all other thoughts and alternatives from his mind except doing exactly as Sam had told him to do. As insurance, however, Sam had a "made" man from Mountain Bell sitting on a tap covering Arnie's phone and both pay booths nearest Arnie's apartment. Sam also had a man sitting in the back seat of Arnie's car, armed with a shotgun, in case Arnie felt the urge to drive downtown to the police or FBI offices.

Harmon Robey and Stephen Ray finished checking their route, traffic flow, sun position, hour, distances, the drop, and the car Sam provided shortly after 3 p.m. Thursday afternoon, an inconspicous '68 brown four-door Chevrolet Chevelle with Utah license plates. Good tires, recent tuneup, no lag when Robey jammed his foot down and hit passing gear, all satisfactory. They would make at least two more run-throughs tomorrow, but he felt ready and right about the score and ready for a drink and dinner. Tomorrow they would move out of The Sundowner, plant sprouts in the desk clerk's, and bell captain's, and maitre d's, and waiters' minds. . . . Couple of solid citizens, quiet, expensively dressed, driving a Mark IV, finished their business and went home, registration card reading Sana Monica, California, with California plates on the car. . . .

Thursday morning Stryker revised the Fugitive Squad's work schedule and made no secret that he did so for purely personal reasons. He put himself and Bellon on evening watch beginning next day. Stryker's motives were two-fold: first, he'd had all his wife's bitching he cared for and could stand, about the heat, never getting a day off, nine hundred things needing repairs around the house; and his daughter Colleen had started wondering who the huge stranger was when Colin came home occasionally. . . . Second, because it was cooler on evening watch than on day watch. With the exception of Ludd, a chronic complainer who'd bitch about getting hung with new rope, men on the Squad were delighted by the change.

When they finished up their last reports, well after 5 p.m., more than an hour after official quitting time, Stryker and Chino dropped by The Sundowner for a couple tall cool ones. They had the third before them, and Chino listened while Stryker told the old joke about the three biggest lies in the world, when the two guys walked into the lounge.

"Don't turn around," Bellon said. "Can you see them in the mirror?"

"Just barely. Why?"

"A couple of wrong sumbitches, Col."

"I'll get some cigars." Stryker slid out of the booth against the back wall and strode toward the cashier. An alert waiter, knowing Stryker's identity, moved fast to serve him. Stryker stopped and positioned himself so he could look past the waiter and see the men, while he told the waiter, "Bring me a couple cigars, any kind. Keep smiling and listening and bobbing your head. See those dudes— no! don't look!—who just came in? Find out if they are registered here. If they are, get the dope off the card, names, addresses, car, and write it down. Bring it to the table with the cigars."

"*A sus ordenes, jefe,*" the waiter said. "At your orders, chief." He took the $5 Stryker handed him, openly; then he turned toward the door and Stryker went back to table, speaking as he dropped down: "So right, pard. Outlaws. You make either of them off our sheets?"

Bellon shook his head: No. He took a swallow of his drink then got up and went to the jook and dropped in three quarters, punched buttons, watched the two men in the back bar reflection. Assholes. Each wore $1000 worth of clothes, but they were still assholes. He knew the look, the style, the manner and dress and attitudes and attributes; what little he had not known, because he was a natural-born cop, Bellon had learned from Stryker since going to Fugitive. The pair of assholes he saw in the mirror reflection were not only assholes but queer for each other. He punched the last button and returned to the table. "OK, you told me the third biggest lie in the world—any nigger can vote in Mississippi. What's second and first?"

"Second biggest: let's stop and have just *one* drink!" They both laughed, and Bellon said, "That's us, huh!"

"And the biggest lie in the world is—now, darlin', I'll just put the head of it in."

They roared, but while they laughed Ballon looked into Stryker's eyes, and he nodded twice, quickly. They drank up, and Stryker held up two fingers. The bartender grinned and got fresh, tall glasses. As he did this, Stryker muttered, "I'm getting a rundown on them from Carlosito."

A few minutes after the bartender set the fresh drinks upon the bar between the chromed out-thrust curved pipes which partitioned the bar so waiters and waitresses could get to the bar for pickups, the waiter named Carlosito, Little Carl, returned and got the drinks, showing the cigars ostentatiously, and came to their table. He leaned over to place the glasses on fresh napkins and put down the cigars, speaking in Spanish, "Inside jacket pocket."

Bellon plucked the stiff paper out and dropped it into his lap. "We'll catch you later," Chino said in Spanish, *"y mil gracias,* a thousand thanks."

"Su seguro servidor, señor, your obedient servent," Little Carl said, backing away.

They peeled cellophane from the cigars and lit up, neither man inhaling. Bellon slid around a few inches so Stryker's massive shape blocked the view of the big man in the booth facing Chino. He slipped the card from his lap and put it on the table as he said, "I got a good look at both and don't make either." He looked down and read from the card, a tab on which Carlosito had written the information:

Harmon and Stephen Robey, 17310 Sunset Blvd., Santa Monica, Calif. Blk Mk IV, lic # 637 ROB.

After a glance, absorbing the information, Chino read aloud in a murmur. As he read the address, Stryker said, "Hold on."

"Huh?"

"That's a phony address."

"Aw, come on, Col. . . . You know the LA area that well?"

"I know the address of the Santa Ynez Inn because Doris and I spent two weeks there when I came back from Nam last tour before I went down t' Pendelton for release from active duty. It's not even in Santa Monica; it's in Pacific Palisades. Anything on there about phone calls?"

"They have direct outside lines and don't list incoming."

"Shit!"

"Let's take'm down, Col."

"On what? Hiway mopery with intent to gawk?"

"Let's hustle the room."

Stryker pondered a moment. The morality did not bother him; he never considered it. He only considered getting caught during an illegal search, which could—technically—be called burglary and certainly *was* unlawful entry, B&E. Finally, he shook his head: No. "It's crapping too close to the house, with them here. We're liable to step in our own shit."

"And track it up the front steps of the police station," Bellon sighed. "OK, what?"

"I give up. What?"

"That's a couple wrong sumbitches, Col. Exactly the kind a guys we wrote the paper on. They're in town for a hit or I'll eat a mile of that pavement."

"Bought, pard. But how does it pay out?"

"I'd bet my hat'n ass they're carrying iron."

"They both got holes in them, pard. Your hat'n ass!"

"Col. . . ."

"Look, you *can't* want the sumbitches more'n I do! But what's the point in spooking them, running them under cover? There's no way we can hold them. They'd bond out. Or their finger man would do so. They're made of rubber, man. We'd need twelve hours for a complete checkout *if* we got an authorization for unlimited use of the telex, which we sure wouldn't, on our goddam budget."

"So?"

"Stay on them. I'm gonna call the old lady and tell her not to wait supper. Get Carlosito over, order chow so this booze don't blow our skulls. I want a double order of red enchiladas with sauce hot enough to burn my ass wrong side out when I crap tomorrow. You'd better get the same. Sober you up like a cold shower shrivels your dick."

Stryker slid out of the booth and went out of the lounge to the pay phone in the hallway, on the way between the lounge and lobby, and called his wife. Chino gave Carlosito the high sign and stuffed a $10 bill in his empty glass while he held the big menu up, concealing the glass. He spoke entirely in Spanish, "Keep bringing drinks in tall glasses, but cut the booze in half. We want chow, hot, *chili colorado y jalepenos,* greasy beans to absorb the booze. Bring two double seltzers like drinking water, eh? And keep your eye on those *maricónes.* If they leave, follow them; we'll make it right with your boss or let him soak in the fuckin slammer!"

"Segurísimo, jefe, como se dice, exácto! Absolutely, chief, exactly as you say!"

Bellon put on his own gameface, what he'd learned from Stryker but not yet refined. *"No me chínges, Carlosito, como rajón, eh?* Don't try fucking me around like a cowardly untrustworthy incest-committing lying cheat eh?"

"Absolutamente no, jefe, nunca te chingo. Aquí vivo yo, y los maricónes son estranjeros qué no debo nada, nada, nada, incluyente mis huevos sudorientos. Beyond the slightest question of doubt, chief, I would never fuck over you. I live in this town, and those queers are strangers, pas-

sers-through whom I owe nothing, nothing, nothing at all, including the sweat off my balls."

"I will remember, and Little Carl— tell the cashier, we may have to leave fast, without paying, eh? Tell her she must cause no commotion. Under my plate or Stryker's will be money." Chino smiled and then resumed his gameface. 'If she does not like that, then I will go now to the telephone and summon the state liquor control agents to check the ages of certain customers I now see drinking beer."

"As you wish, chief; you're the boss. I don't think it necessary, any phone calls. She will cooperate." Carlosito grinned. "One of you. . ." He kept grinning and made an in-and-out movement with the palms of his hands facing Chino, knuckles bent down, the old Mexican gesture for making love. Some cop was bedding the cashier.

"Tengo hambre," Chino said, dropping the gameface and smiling. "I'm hungry."

"You want the *botana?" Botana* being Spanish for snacks, *hors d'oeuvres.*

"Get it on, man!"

Little Carl left after plucking the $10 from Chino's glass and secreting it, writing on his ticket pad. As he went to the kitchen window, Stryker came back into the lounge. He did not look at the men in the booth.

Stephen Ray sat facing the door and saw Stryker enter; he nodded. Robey did not move but cut his blue eyes so he saw Stryker from the corner of his eye the instant he came into range. Robey had never seen many men he feared on sight, possibly two, perhaps five, during his entire life. But he felt a sensation which he recognized as fear when he looked at Stryker, and after thinking it through, he realized he feared the man simply because looking at Stryker was the same as looking at himself, with a single exception. . . . the huge cop wasn't gay.

That the enormous son of a bitch wore a thin gold wedding band meant nothing to Robey; he just knew; he should, after all these years. . . .

69

Robey lifted his glass so it shielded his face and said, "They're cops and they've made us."

He saw the sheer undiluted fright gloss Steve's eyes. He was a lovely punk, but he only knew the dealing end of horror and death: he'd never faced it himself, been tested, put to the fire, tempered, made strong and tough. Robey watched dispassionately while Steve reached . . . and finally got hold of himself, controlling his fear and trigger-quick emotions. "Harmon . . . what are we going to do?"

"Wait."

"I don't know if I can."

"You can do anything I *tell* you, Steve . . . can't you?"

"I'll try."

"No try. *Do!*"

"All right, darl—Harmon."

"Can you see them in the mirror?"

"Only from an angle."

"Use it. They *must* be the pair Sam wants iced."

"I agree." Steve squirmed in his seat. "Harmon, I've never seen anyone that large before, except when you took me to see the Rams and Cowboys play."

"And you hooked up with that bastard from the Rams."

"You're not still angry about that, darling, surely."

"I like to know where you are, Steve . . . in case we get a call."

"I made a promise and I'll keep it. Never again!"

"Are you watching?"

"Actually, no."

"I suggest you do. . . . Because I see now what Sam meant. This may be a hick town, comparatively; but that's as badass a pair of badges as I've ever seen. They'd render us in a minute. They'd kick in our door and blow us up and throw Saturday Night Specials down beside us if they didn't find our own iron."

Robey never looked directly at Bellon, who faced him, nor at the back of Stryker's head. He sat and considered and revolved the plans through his mind, and again; and he found no flaw; but he did see the tiny chicano waiter keep taking drink after drink to the cops' table, and that worried him. They could get stoned, and just for the hell of it, because they were both such big, stout, arrogant bastards, decide they'd better roust the fruiters. Without preamble, Robey told Steve, "Go to the room. Before you go in, get the shotguns from the car."

"Wha—!"

"Shut *up!* Just *go!*"

Steve came to his feet and shot out of the booth as though he had springs in his butt and in seconds left the lounge. Robey watched the face of the cop he could see, and to his amazement saw no change of expression on the dark, oriental-looking face. Robey wondered if he was wrong. He kept watching, zeroing in on the man's lips, waiting for him to speak, but he did not. He kept stuffing food into his mouth with both hands, reminiscent of Sam Borchia.

Robey could not believe he'd been that wrong. Those bastards were *cops!* He felt it, he *knew!* and yet . . . Robey summoned the waiter, added the tab carefully, signed his name and room number and left a cheap tip. As he walked out, he casually looked into the mirror and watched.

Neither of the men he *knew* were cops paid him the slightest attention. As he walked out of the lobby and turned toward his room, Robey felt confusion. He could not possibly be so wrong. He walked on down the paved central area, then ducked between parked cars. He waited thirty minutes. Neither man came into view. Finally Robey shrugged, turned, and went to the room. He rapped on the door, once, twice, once. Steve opened the door and stepped back, swirling his kimono. . . .

71

6—FUBAR

Robey could not shake his feeling about the men in the lounge the night before. During his first runthrough next morning, Robey's erratic driving almost earned him a traffic ticket. His mood was murderous. The motorcycle cop would never know he'd barely escaped a lethal confrontation only because he had orders to investigate a reported Signal 82—motor vehicle collision, injured persons—and passed up Robey's dangerous lane-changing violation because the call had priority.

Steve became increasingly nervous and finally asked, "Harmon, what *is* it?"

"Shut up, punk."

They did not speak as Robey returned to the motel. He parked the Chevelle in the driveway. "Get our gear packed. I'll check us out." He left the brown car, slamming the door, then shoved past a waiter just inside the lobby. "Get out of the way, spic!"

Carlos Baca looked narrowly at the man and recognized him. He straightened his white bumfreezer and shot a look at the driveway. The sight of the young queer behind the wheel of a nondescript old Chevy made him start. Carlosito turned and walked past the desk where the big man stood facing the clerk. Carlos went to the lounge, stepped behind the bar, picked up the telephone, and dialed 911.

The policewoman at the complaint board at the police station explained she could not transfer his call, that all offices, bureaus, departments, divisions, etc. had individual numbers. Carlos finally got the Fugitive Squad number, hungup, and dialed. Stryker was not in nor expected till 2:30 p.m., possibly later, for evening watch duty. Carlos asked for Stryker's home telephone number, and the cop on the other end of the line laughed before saying, "We don't give out that dope, feller."

"This important, and I, well . . . I work with Stryker, you know?"

"Then you should have his number."

"You gonna be sorry, man, I don't get him right now, soon!"

"Yeah?" The detective laughed again. "Sue me! Or tell me. I'm a cop."

"I don't wanna talk to no one but Stryker or Bellon."

"You're still outta luck. Bellon and Stryker work partners."

"What's your name, man.? I'm gonna report you, this's important."

"Dick Tracy—that's my fuckin name!" Southerlund shouted. "Now, look, I told you—I'm a cop, too. I'm here *now*. You want help, tell me. You have information, tell me. Otherwise, get the hell off this line and let me get back to work."

"Can I leave a number and my name? You know, then you call Stryker at home and have him call me back?"

"Yeah, yeah, OK!"

"Tell him he should call Carlosito at work, right away, very important, about those two guys last night."

"What guys?"

"Stryker or Bellon will know. If you can't reach Stryker, try Chino, OK, Mr. Detective Dick Tracy?"

"Yeah, sure," said Detective Gene Southerlund and hung up. Southerlund did not write down the message. Screw that smartass spic. He yawned, shot a look at the door, made sure it was closed with a chair blocking it, then Southerlund leaned back and resumed his nap. Friggin spics, gettin' so they think they're good as a white man, bastards. . . .

Stryker mowed the front lawn with Colleen riding on his shoulders, chattering, kicking her tiny feet into his chest, teasing he'd missed this or that spot. He finished and shut the mower off, swung his daughter down, and she

73

walked beside him, bumping his leg as he shoved the machine toward the storage shed at the end of the open carport.

Colleen stopped and placed her hands on her hips in a perfect imitation of her mother when Doris became exasperated. "What about the back grass, Dad?"

"Not today, boss. I've had it."

"It's not even lunchtime yet."

"It's beertime, though."

Her face squeezed up in a tight grin and she took off, running as hard as she could, and stopped two inches from the back door, just as it seemed impossible to avoid colliding. She reached up, opened the door, went inside, letting the screen slam. Stryker put the mower away and locked the storage shed. Then he went into the kitchen. Colleen had a bottle of Michelob out of the refrigerator and an opener. She ran at him. He caught her and swooped her high into the air, looking into her dark blue green eyes, still amazed at the miracle of birth.

She was so small he could hold her bottom in one big hand, out to the side, while she swung her legs and kept her balance, a perfectly formed toylike creature, who was not a toy but a real, live *person*.

Stryker held her high, and Colleen reached the ceiling with her opener and the beer. He let her drop breathlessly almost past his waist, then caught her again and set her upon the kitchen table. He took the beer and looked at it critically. "With all that shaking, it'll be nothing but foam."

"I like foam best, Dad."

"Well, I guess this one's yours, then."

"Dad, you mean the *whole* thing?"

"You watch too much TV."

"But, Dad, the *whole* thing?" She giggled and turned so she looked at him with just the corner of her right eye.

"I feel sorry for the boys when *you* grow up, kid. Where'd you learn all the moves, anyway?"

"Well, Dad, after all, I'm almost five."

"*That* is an exaggeration, young lady. You won't be five for another seven months."

"Well, four'n a half."

"Exaggeration."

"Dad, are you going to open my beer?"

"That's right, change the subject." Stryker shook his head. He looked at her a moment longer, feeling love come uprushing in his throat, then he picked her up and kissed her cheek. He put her down and took the bottle to the sink, tilted and opened it, clamping the heel of his hand over the foaming beer, then tipped it farther and released his hand, let the foam gush into Colleen's big plastic personal and private mug. When the mug filled, Stryker brought the bottle to his lips and drank deeply, finishing off the beer, getting a headache above his right eye. Colleen had a white foam moustache, holding her mug in both hands.

"Believe I will, kid," Stryker said, pulling off a long strip of paper towels and swabbing down his face and neck and bare torso. "And don't foam it all up."

Colleen put down her mug and brought another beer, carefully, in both hands. Stryker took it and kissed her forehead, opened the beer, carried it to the kitchen table. He pulled down the wall phone and dialed, then sat down and drank while the number rang.

"Ah, hello?"

"Christ, sounds like you kept going after I left you last night."

"Friend of mine came over."

"Can you talk?"

"Yeah, she's in the kitchen rustling up some grub."

"Anyone I know?"

"Nope."

"How do you know?"

"I don't screw my boss's old girlfriends."

"You heard anything?"

Ní una palabra," Bellon said, "not a single word."

"You check in with the office?"

"Nope."

"I'm just fixing to call. Hang in there till I get back to you, OK?"

"I'll be here."

Stryker hung up and drank two long swallows, then dialed his office. Stryker frowned when the phone rang three times. Then it was picked up, dropped clattering, and a coarse, husky voice finally answered, "Fugitive, uh, ah, um, Fugitive Squad, Southerlund."

"You awake yet, Fubar?"

"Sure, skipper; I just got a hell of a sinus stoppage."

"Shit, Southerlund, you were crapped out again."

"Now, skip—"

"Forget the shuck. I had any calls, or Bellon?"

A silence came on the line.

At the other end Southerlund estimated his chances. It seemed clear now he'd made a serious mistake not forwarding the message from that wiseass meskin, and it would be a gut cinch for Stryker to check back and find who'd been on phone watch in the office. Southerlund also knew from long experience that a complete admission of minor wrongdoing disarmed superiors, left them with nothing they could use to rake his ass over the grate with, so he got a half-hearted assreaming and by efficiency report time nothing showed up in his file in writing, so he got his annual paygrade and longevity raises. Putting an extra touch of country-stupid on his words, Southerlund said: "Sumbitch, skipper, I *did* get a call in here fo you'er Chino; but I got busier'n a one-legged man at a asskickin contest and plumb forgot. Goddam phone's been ringin off the desk."

"Yeah, sure, you dipshit. . . .Well, what's the message?"

Stryker pulled a pad and pencil stub from a small shelf under the wallphone.

Southerlund could not remember the caller's name. "He wanted your home number, skip, which I know ain't allowed—"

"Southerlund, just cut the crap. If I know you, you were too friggin lazy or half-asleep and didn't write the message down. . . . So tell me what you remember."

"It was some wiseass spic, and he didn't give a name, trying to play secret agent, you know? I told him—"

"Never fuckin mind what *you* told *him!* I want the message." Stryker had dozens of informants, throughout the

76

city and the state, in every state bordering New Mexico, in California and Vegas and the Pacific Northwest; he had no idea who'd called, nor about what; but he did know one thing: he was shipping that sorryass Southerlund. If Auto Theft or General Assignment or Burglary could not use him, then back to uniform; he'd make a hell of a school crossing guard, if he didn't fall asleep on his feet.

"He said tell you it was about some guys last night."

"Son of a bitch! How long ago did he call?"

"Oh, not long," Southerlund lied. "I been so busy I—"

"*Suuure,* you have. Listen, I'm calling the dispatcher and sending Zenner in to relieve you. I want someone dependable on phone watch. You better get down the hallway and see if you can politic yourself a job someplace else in detective division because I'm shipping your worthless ass the end of the month."

Stryker slammed down the phone, redialed Chino, and told him to saddle up. He called the complaint board and got hold of the detective division dispatcher and gave instructions. He got the phone book down and dialed The Sundowner, asked for Carlos Baca, and was told Carlos had already left for his afternoon break and would not return until 4 p.m. Stryker asked for Harmon Robey's room. "I'm sorry, sir; the Robeys checked out some two hours ago."

"And left no forwarding address, I suppose."

"I'm sorry, sir, no."

Stryker thanked the woman and hung up, cursing silently. Fubar Southerlund. *F*ucked *U*p *B*eyond *A*ll *R*emedies. Fubar. . . .

Robey pulled the Chevelle alongside the curb two blocks past the parking lot and Steve got in. "He went for it when I gave him the sawbuck," Steve said and held up the keys to the Mark IV. "He didn't stamp a ticket and stub."

Robey smiled. "I told you it would work."

Steve nodded. "What some people will do for money."

They both laughed aloud. Robey had contrived the story, and Steve carried it through: he wanted to hide the Mark IV because his wife had discovered he was in the city, and she had a paper to take possession of the IV because he was so far behind in alimony payments. He would return and get the car after finishing his business that evening. In the meantime, he wanted no record of where he'd hidden—you know?

The pimply faced youth with nasty hair and green teeth grinned widely and pocketed the $10, guided Steve to the last row, and showed him where to park. "There won't be nobody on duty after eight tonight and I have to lock the gate, but I'll put on a combination lock so you can get in with these numbers." He gave Steve a slip of paper on which he'd scrawled, R-20, L-5, R-11.

"You do a lot of this?"

"Jist say it ain't the first time I helped a guy. . . ."

As Robey drove the Chevelle off Central and up a ramp leading onto I-25, Steve said, "For ten bucks the idiot could lose every car on the lot, Harmon. I mean, what if putting the Mark IV on the lot and that story on him was only a shuck?"

"He'd protect himself. He'd have a broken lock lying on the ground for the cops to see."

"It's still stupid."

"All smallbore thieves are stupid, Steve."

78

Robey felt better, now things began falling into place. He exited from the freeway and slowed, then pulled in at a small, inconspicuous motel.

Robey registered them as H. Robeson and party, Moab, Utah. The elderly owner never saw Steve, only a shape sitting in the car, and Robey had altered his appearance: he had not shaved that morning or combed his sweaty and rumpled hair; he wore wraparound sunglasses and a short-sleeved sports shirt, tail out.

He paid in advance, telling the clerk they would not stay the night; they only wanted the room for a few hours so they could rest up before going on home, delighting the clerk. If they cleared out soon enough, he could whip on clean sheets, empty the ashtrays, wipe out the used glasses before wrapping plastic around them, then rent the room again for full price and pocket the money.

They carried everything into the room, turned on the air conditioner and TV. While Steve showered and shaved, Robey worked over their firearms: the two revolvers, an AR-15 automatic rifle, and two automatic shotguns—a pair of Ithaca Featherweight 20-gauge which had been sawed off at both barrel and stock ends so the guns were only 21½ inches long; the plugs had been removed from the magazines so each gun held six rounds, counting that in the chamber. Before he broke the guns down, Robey put on a pair of new medical gloves so he would leave no fingerprints, even on the inner parts or the ammunition.

Stryker and Bellon hit the streets in the gray Ford at 1:45 p.m. They drove directly to Carlos Baca's apartment, having gotten the address from the dining room manager. Carlos was not home. Indeed, his wife seemed astonished the police thought they might find Carlos at home in the middle of a working day. They did not push it. Carlos evidently had a little something going on the side and had never told his wife he got an afternoon break from 1 to 4 p.m. They did not exactly blame Carlos. Chino said, as they got back into the Ford, "Man, you could sing that old song, *You Ain't Nothin' But A Hound-dog* to her and be right on, couldn't you?"

"Looks like she's been eating ugly pills, all right."

"What'd you figure she'd dress out? One ninety, two hundred?"

"Close enough."

Back at the motel, they learned nothing from anyone on duty. Feeling quite certain Carlos had no homo tendencies, they got the names and addresses of all female employees who had the same afternoon break hours and began calling those who had home telephones, not asking if Carlos was there, but if they'd heard him say where he was going that afternoon. Bellon used another line and notified Zenner on phone watch in Fugitive office. They drove to the homes of two women whose personnel files did not list a home telephone. Neither was home.

Stryker looked at Bellon, and Bellon stared back, and they both shrugged. They returned to the motel bar and had a drink, with nothing to do but wait for Carlosito's return.

An employee of The Man in Phoenix, after several attempts, finally reached Sam Borchia at the meat packers. Sam went out to a pay telephone with two rolls of quarters and called another pay phone in Scottsdale. The Man answered. Sam listened, and Sam agreed with The Man, not only because he had no choice in the matter regardless of what his own preferences might or might not be, but because he believed as sincerely as The Man did that this was unquestionably the most logical and intelligent and safest move they could make.

Sam hung up and went back to his office, cleaned up his work, drove out to the home occupied by one of the former legbreakers. Sam and the crippled man secluded themselves in the den after the man sent his wife and children shopping with $50 Sam slipped him. After listening, the cripple said, "I don't see how we can handle it, Sam." He shook his head. "Sure, me'n Tony can blow'm up, no sweat. But without help . . . no way we can collect the loot and get the bodies loaded and the hell out of there."

"Joseph, I'm not asking anything impossible. I know what you can't do. I only want to know if you will take the contract?"

"Sure."

"I'll have Tony back in town by five-thirty. Have your wife drive you over, be there at the same time, five-thirty, got that?"

"Sure, Sam."

"It goes down a few minutes before six, but I don't know when those fuckin queers'll show; they keep everything tight. I doubt you should expect them before midnight. But maybe by nine or ten. You'll just have to sweat it out."

"I haven't forgot how, Sam."

"Good!" Sam touched Joe's arm. "In case you're wondering, we have orders on this from Arizona."

Joe shook his head. "I work for you, Sam; you've taken care of me since—" Joe looked down at his useless legs. "I don't give a rat's ass about any Arizona orders, just what *you* say!"

"You a good boy, Joe; you'n Tony both good boys; you'll never want for anything so long as Sam Borchia's alive."

"I know that, Sam; and thanks. . . . And I hope we can set something up on—you know. . . ." Joe looked down at his fixed, permanently bent, fused knee joints, and tears dribbled down his cheeks.

"We will, Joey; we will. I made you a promise. You know I'll keep it."

"Sure, Sam."

"We got to be careful, that's all. Hit that Bellon greaser sumbitch too soon, and they trace it right back to us. Revenge ain't worth going to the joint for, Joey."

"I know, Sam; but I hope it's soon, real soon. I live for the day I'll watch that lousy bastard squirm." It never occured to Joey or Sam or the absent Tony (nor would have to the now dead "Scatter-bone" who'd driven the Mercury that night) that Bellon had only defended himself, then

81

taken out insurance by making absolutely sure neither Tony nor Joseph could ever call on him with ballbats again. In their world, with its goals and objectives, morality, and set of values, a victim simply had no right whatever to fight back; that a chosen victim should not only fight back but overcome them and savage them, leaving them as they intended to leave the victim, was simply beyond their comprehension. The game was not played that way: it violated their rules, had so enraged Sam he'd made that telephone call, which he acknowledged had been stupid. . . . If you intend revenge, warning the man in advance is hardly wise; it is, in fact, stupid!

Arrangements made, Sam drove directly to his construction company warehouse, entered a concealed vault, and got two handguns equipped with silencers. He put the weapons in a toolbox and locked it, gave the Negro janitor a key to Tony's house, and the black man delivered the weapons, placing the toolbox on the kitchen table of the vacant home. Sam took the key back and gave the janitor the rest of the day off.

Then Sam went into his office and closed the door and sat behind his desk for twenty minutes, thinking. At last he regretfully made his decision. Joey and Tony had become dangerous; they brooded over their crippled legs; Joe's tears showed him undependable, near cracking. If the fuzz got hold of Joe now, he'd send the whole organization up in a sheet of flaming publicity in spite of Sam's attempts at avoiding this by providing for Joe and Tony more than adequately—good homes in fine neighborhoods with excellent schools and fire and police protection, a new car every other year, an income. . . .

But Joe had cracked, so he must be taken care of, and no use putting off Tony. Ice them both at the same time in Tony's place, scatter evidence around so the cops and feds would conclude Joe and Tony fingered the bank job, then had a gunfight over the split. That meant leaving the little bitch's, Steve's, body in the house, and taking Robey's out and throwing it down a mineshaft or dropping various dissected parts into remote cañons from an airplane. The

82

hands would have to be burned or fed to the dogs, so Robey's fingerprints could never be traced, and his teeth removed and pulverized so there could never be a dental check. With consideration of these details, Sam moved well beyond any feeling of compassion, regret, or remorse that he might have felt about Tony and Joe. They had served long and faithfully but were no longer of any use to him; they had in fact become definite liabilities.

That reminded Sam he had one other detail which required his attention. He called Witterstadt and gave him new instructions. Sam looked at his watch, then went out and drove to a telephone booth and, at the agreed time, the phone rang. Robey told him the name and location of the motel they'd moved into. "Room sixteen. It's crummy but suits our purpose better than a carpet joint. The place has a switchboard, so don't call unless it's cancelled out for some reason, and then just say, *Red said forget it*. OK?"

"Perfect. I just checked in out there, and it's all set."

"No changes at all?"

"None," Sam lied, "exactly the way I laid it out for you guys the other night."

"It had better be."

Sam made no reply; he smiled as he wiped his face, sweating heavily in the stifling phone booth.

"You left the envelope for your split?"

"Yeah," Sam said, "Tony taped it behind the toilet tank like you said do."

"We're all set. We won't see you again, so thanks. Maybe we can do business together again."

"Why not, a couple nice polite guys like you."

"Look—"

Sam hung up and stepped out of the booth, wiping his face, walked back to his Cadillac, and turned the air conditioning full blast after starting the motor. As he drove, he went back over the details of his revised plan. . . . He had everything covered.

Carlosito showed up fifteen minutes late and smelling

like a zoo. "I hope you had a good time, you little asshole," Stryker said.

"I gotta shower and change fast, man; I'm already late."

"So it can wait a few minutes longer," Bellon said. "What's up?"

"They got another car, those fruits last night."

Bellon flipped his notepad open, "*Dígame,* spill it!"

"A Cheevee, four doors, brown, Utah plates, I don't know the numbers."

"Couldn't you walk *fifty* yards?" Stryker snapped.

"I came right away and called. Say, who's that smartass call hisself Dick Tracy?"

"Get the hell *on* with it!"

"I called right away I saw the big guy checking out and the punk driving the other car. I talked to that Dick Tracy, but he won't give me your number or Chino's and only say, *yeah, yeah,* or something like that, smartass, when I say call you and have you call me. I wait and wait for the ring but never come, and the boss on my ass get my sidework done or no afternoon break, so I went back to work. When I get a chance I look again, both cars gone."

"Craphouse mouse!" Bellon said through his teeth.

"Milk it," Stryker told Chino and turned abruptly away. He called Zenner in the office. "Is that assfaced Southerlund still around?"

"He's not here in the office, and I've been sticking by the phone, skipper."

"While you're doing that, type an official departmental complaint against Southerlund, failure to follow established practices, procedures, routines, and conduct unbecoming. Sign my name by you. I'll call John The Baptist and tell him you're sending it. I want Southerlund served with that complaint and indefinite suspension before he leaves the building if possible."

"Check, skipper. What'n hell did he *do?* This time?"

Stryker ignored the question. "*First,* get out an all-city broadcast—" Stryker gave Zenner descriptions of the cars and men. "Have the dispatcher emphasize, however, subjects are *not,* say again, *not* to be stopped, but only placed under surveillance."

"OK, I got that. . . . Southerlund just came in, skip. You wanna talk to him?"

"You bet I do!"

"Yeah, skip, what's up?"

"You are. This is official notification, Southerlund. You are hereby suspended indefinitely. Report to Deputy Chief Seamon. He will take your credentials and badge and serve you with the papers."

Stryker did not allow Southerlund to answer. He hung up, dialed the DC's office, and told Seamon what he could expect in the next few minutes. Seamon wanted details, but Stryker put him off. "I'm working a hot case right now, and Zenner can fill you in." He hung up and went back. Bellon shook his head. "Not another drop. He gave all his milk down first time through."

"Then let's start looking for those friggin cars."

8—RIPOFF

As the days closed in upon him, Chief of Security Arnold Witterstadt became almost insane with anxiety. He quit eating as the only way he could stop spending hours in the toilet every day. He lived on coffee and cigarettes, though his guts cramped and seethed worse than ever; and from new pains high up under his diaphragm, the vagus nerve, he knew he'd developed one hell of an ulcer. But at least he could now safely pass wind with little fear of soiling his drawers.

By the time Sam Borchia called on *the* day, Witterstadt was in such a neurotic state he never questioned Sam's minor change in plans, that he should stand by at the back door and help the gunmen load the car. All Witterstadt could think was, *tonight it will all be over!*

He had no premonition how right he was. All his problems had been solved, permanently.

Almost in a state of euphoria, at twelve minutes before six, Arnold made his customary tour around the bank lobby, speaking the same words to each guard, "On your toes now, this and opening time are the most dangerous."

Each guard, sick of hearing it, grunted or nodded or said, "Yeah, chief, right on."

Arnold finished his check at ten before six and went out of the lobby toward the back door. He stopped in the hallway, opened the locked small door set into the wall, took the special key, and switched off the alarm system. He did not fully close the door, but left it slightly ajar so he would not have to reopen it while under great stress and crowded for time. Thinking ahead, Arnold removed the alarm system key from his keyring and left it in the switch.

Then he walked on toward the back door and slipped the latch, at eight minutes before six. He went back along the hallway and through a door which let him in behind the counter. The wheeled cart upon which the tellers placed their locked drawer trays and/or heavy canvas pouches stood ready for the vault.

Arnold asked, "All ready?" His voice sounded cracked and nervous in his own ears, but no one looked at him curiously. Without waiting for an answer, Arnold grabbed the trunk's handles and shoved. The greased wheels moved easily despite the weight. Arnold rolled the truck out and down the hallway, speeded up as he looked at his watch saw it was *time*. . . .

The robbery went down at precisely six minutes before 6 p.m., precisely as planned . . . with one slight variation.

Dressed as they had been in Phoenix and all other jobs, Robey and Ray came through the back door, armed with automatic shotguns in their hands, revolvers in waist holsters, stocking masks over their faces, medical gloves on their hands.

Then occurred the slight variation.

Robey staggered with astonishment for an instant when he jerked open the back door and found Witterstadt standing there close with a slight nervous smile on his thick lips.

Robey shot a hole through Witterstadt's middle with the shotgun at a range of some three feet.

Though he was far stronger and should load the heavy trays and pouches, Robey had no faith Steve could stand off the other guards. He shouted, *"Load it!"* and shoved another round into the shotgun. When the first guard charged around the corner at the end of the hallway, Robey held fire. Then came a second and a third. Robey unloaded on them, three shots as fast as he could pull off. The guards went down, one getting off a single wild shot that ricocheted screamingly along the stone floor and concrete walls.

Robey reloaded without looking as he shot a glance over his shoulder. Steve stood there with his mouth open, eyes glazed; Robey saw even through the stocking mask. He whipped the shotgun barrel across Steve's side, popping a rib. *"Load it, goddam you!"*

Steve broke free of the stark immobilizing fear and shoved the truck out the back door and against the rear bumper of the Chevelle. He began throwing trays and pouches into the trunk, its decklid up, ready.

Loading became too slow and difficult with one hand, so Ray put his shotgun on the rear fender and used both hands, throwing the trays and pouches into the trunk. He heard Harmon fire again, and again, but he did not look; he kept loading.

Then suddenly Harmon came alongside him, hit him hard, shouting, *"Let's go!"*

Steve became aware that the alarm had started ringing. He slammed down the trunk lid and ran to the open right front door. He barely made it inside as Harmon jerked the Chevelle into gear and jammed his foot to the floor. He drove with both hands until they hit the street, then with one hand while he ripped the stocking from his head. Steve followed suit. Less than two minutes later they joined the short line leading into a drive-in movie. By one minute past six, Harmon had paid the cashier and driven inside, parked three rows behind the projection booth. He reached under the seat and brought out a bottle of bourbon, twisted the cap off and upended it, taking two long swallows.

Clenching his teeth so he would not sob, Steve said, "My god, Harmon, what *happened?*"

"Fuck'f I know, kid. It looked like a set-up, but now I don't think it was; at least not for us. For that guard. Sam wanted him blown up, didn't trust him, I guess. It's probably best; he looked weak."

"Are all the others dead, too?"

"I don't know. Fuck'm. That one stupid bastard. Not *his* money, probably makes ninety or a hundred a week. I already unlegged him, but he's gotta be a fuckin hero, crawling up the wall, turned the alarm switch, damn fool, he's dead now." Robey took another long swallow. The whisky burned down his gullet. He turned toward Steve and smiled and then felt his face tighten as his gaze searched without finding. "Where's your shotgun?"

"Oh, *god!*"

"Meaning *what?*"

"We lost it, back at the bank."

"What?"

Steve told him the trouble he had had loading with one hand, how he had laid the shotgun on the fender, then forgot it. . . .

"Oh, Harmon, I'm so sorry."

"You think being *sorry's* going to save our asses? You stupid ball-less freak!"

"Does it matter that much?" Steve sobbed.

"I'm trying to remember. Shut *up!*" Robey took another belt. Christ, that had been tight. He tried but could not remember how many men he'd shot. He did not care. He *did* care about being caught, identified. The shotgun . . . OK, he had it now . . . cool, they were cool. He opened the door and held it for a moment. "What do you want?"

"I couldn't eat a bite, dar— Harmon."

Robey went to the snackbar and got three bar-B-Q beefs, two large cold drinks, a double order of onion rings, and a triple-size Styrofoam cup of coffee with a lid on. He carried the food back and got into the Chevelle as the pre-movie cartoons came on, that ace Roadrunner making a fool of the stupid coyote. . . . Me and the cops, Robey thought, sitting down and running the seat back against the stops so he had plenty of room behind the wheel.

He gave Steve one of the sandwiches and a cold drink. "Eat!"

"Harmon, really, I couldn't—"

"Eat! This isn't over yet. It may be a long time between meals. *Eat!"*

Robey turned on the car's radio and listened to the excited announcer's tumbling words. Only one fact meant anything to Robey: ". . .police admit total bafflement as to the gunmen's identity. . . ."

Robey took a huge bit of bar-B-Q and smiled as he chewed and watched the Roadrunner move from under a falling anvil. The anvil had a rope tied around it. The coyote held the end of the rope, too short, it jerked the coyote into the air with the velocity of a rocket launch and ironed him against the side of a solid stone mountain. The anvil missed the Roadrunner and sank out of sight into the earth. The stupid coyote kept hold of the rope, and it jerked his flattened body off the side of the stone mountain and down into the anvil-shaped hole. A moment later the coyote emerged, stunned, tattered, ripped, torn, and totally befuddled.

Robey roared with laughter, continuing to see himself as the Roadrunner and the coyote representing all cops.

He took another huge bit of sandwich and leaned back to enjoy the movies and the meal.

Unfortunately, Robey's imagination hardly differed from events then in progress at The Bank of the Rockies. In actuality, almost none of the cops on the scene fitted the old-movie or coyote cliché: utter stupidity. But they all seemed poorly trained, incompetent, and incapable, thanks partly to the FBI's new Special Agent In Charge—SAIC —H. Ardd Peters.

Recently promoted, short and stout, wearing eyeglasses, his last assignment having ill prepared him for a bank job massacre his second week in the city. Peters tried covering his incompetence by shielding himself behind a facade of angry bluster. His attitude arose from a fundamental cause: he felt intimidated. As peculiar as it may be, the FBI had much the least demanding physical requirements of any agency represented on the scene. With the combination of his incompetence and having to look up to all but two of his own special agents, who were equally short and stout, Peters' mood had become positively virulent, maliciously obnoxious.

Sgt/Det Colin Stryker, utterly unaware of Peters' afflictions, unfortunately chose this particular time to approach the green new SAIC, offer his evaluation of the robbery, and suggest the possibility that Robey and his punk could be involved, for the single surviving bank guard kept insisting the getaway car had been a Chevelle; he knew because he owned one.

SAIC Peters flared at Stryker like a blowtorch, and Stryker stared down at the man with contempt as he spoke; "I don't give a fiddler's fuck about jurisdictional disputes, ace. You and my Superintendent can work out that cheap shit after we've got these bastards in the slammer. I'm offering you the best and *only* truly good lead we have."

Stryker tried explaining. but Peters did not like the direct approach from a lowly sergeant, and since no Inspector or Deputy Chief or Deputy Super had yet arrived on the scene through whom Stryker could relay the information via chain of command, Stryker quit Peters. As he turned away, he spoke distinctly, "Come on, Chino; we'll let the glory grabbing brown-nosers play around here while we *find* the assholes."

To an agent at his side, Peters hissed, "Get that man's name!"

Stryker heard and turned back. "Stryker. S-T-R-Y-K-E-R. Sergeant Detective Colin MacGregor Stryker, commander, Fugitive Squad, badge number ninety-six. Anything else?"

Peters hid behind his facade, acting as though he had not heard Stryker speak.

Stryker grinned meanly. "In case we find them, I promise we won't violate their fuckin rights, at least not so much as they did those men!" Stryker swung his huge catcher's mitt hand toward the sheet-covered stretchers which white-coated men trundled toward waiting ambulances.

Patrolmen W. Southwell and J. Elmore had worked partners for almost eleven years, virtually all of those years in the same district. Both had served in the Navy during the Korean War, Southwell as a hospital corpsman, Elmore as an enlisted aircrewman; both had two years college before coming on the cops. Both had been repeatedly offered detective division assignments over the years and refused. Because they'd started graying at the temples and Elmore's hairline receded, many other cops and citizens of the city, upon seeing them, thought them more or less sub-moronic —men their ages, with a shred of intelligence, should be sergeants, perhaps lieutenants or captains, and most certainly detectives.

In fact, however, Elmore and Southwell loved being cops, uniformed cops, patrolmen. They knew better than most men the absolute truth of the stenciled sign on the wall in the Patrol Division meeting room:

ALL OTHER DIVISIONS IN THIS DEPARTMENT EXIST FOR A SINGLE PURPOSE: TO PERFORM THOSE DUTIES WHICH PATROL DIVISION HAS NO TIME FOR.

They loved the feeling, the knowledge, that for eight hours of every workday, a certain part of the city *belonged* to them, and they belonged to it, both its masters and its servants, Patrol District 21. Theirs! For example, Sam Borchia's loan sharks and bookies and numbers runners did not operate in 21 District, for the simple reason that when Sam moved his assholes in, Southwell and Elmore ran them out. As a matter of fact, Bellon had not pulled Ugly Al Ruga's cherry in this city—Southwell had, two days after Al set up a back office. While Elmore covered the front and downed every asshole who came through the door, Southwell kicked in the back door and took Al down. Al started beefing about his rights, search and seizure, and Southwell fed him the big end of a baton, and while Al lay on the floor wondering where that fuckin truck went that just ran over him, Southwell told him, "I see you in my district again, shitface, and I'll ram this club so far up your ass you'll be lookin' at the world through splinters!"

So Elmore and Southwell considered it a personal affront that *any* assholes should pull a bank job in *their* district. It ate holes in their asses like acid. They listened to the radio, waiting for a description—car, subjects, anything; and finally they recognized Stryker when he switched over on channel one and asked the dispatcher to repeat the earlier broadcast about the Chevelle, the Mark IV, and the two men.

92

Both patrolmen hit upon the realization at almost the exact same instant as they cruised back on the boulevard. Southwell, driving, glanced in the rearview mirror and saw the bank, then looked ahead and saw the drive-in movie. Elmore saw the drive-in movie, then looked back over his shoulder at the bank. They stared at one another, then nodded. Southwell wheeled in and stopped beside the cashier's booth. A teenager came out for the money, saw the police car, then shrugged. Elmore and Southwell got out and went over.

"How long you been on?"

"Since we opened."

"What time?"

"Five-forty-five."

"She been on since then, too?" Southwell jerked his chin toward the plastic blonde with the plastic smile and wig and tits in the booth. "Yeah. What's up?"

"We're looking for a car and a couple guys."

Southwell went to the booth while Elmore questioned the boy. They learned nothing.

They stood beside the car for a moment. "I think it's worth a look."

"Let's go."

They got back into the car and drove in, ignoring the cynical smiles behind them as the cashier and boy thought they were a couple of goof-off cops slipping in to watch a movie.

They cruised the lanes between cars, starting at the back so just in case they *were* right they assholes wouldn't get a look at them driving back and forth along the lanes in front of them.

In the third lane behind the projection booth, at the same instant, both patrolmen said, "That's it."

9—RENDERED

Though both Elmore and Southwell wore the Department Medal of Valor, neither considered himself a hero; the forty-five commendations they'd accumulated over the years meant nothing; they came with the job if men did the job well.

The instant they spotted the car, Southwell braked and Elmore reached for the microphone. "Patrol 21, we've spotted subject car last broadcast in the drive-in movie west of The Bank of the Rockies, standing by."

Robey saw the police car when it entered, but he gave it only a cursory glance and little thought; in fact, he believed the same thing as had the gate people—a couple cops hiding out, "cooping"; catching a few winks or perhaps actually watching the movie, an overly used, ill-lighted, badly spliced print of *The Last Picture Show*.

Robey took another belt of whiskey, chased it with a sip of cold drink, then bit into the second sandwich. His attention drifted from the movie, and he glanced into the rearview mirror. He saw a car passing down the lane several rows behind, and then someone in a car opened the door, silhouetting the gumball atop the police car.

Robey sat up, turned, and looked. The police car pulled into a vacant spot beside a speaker and stopped; he saw the red, glowing brakelights. He faced the screen again and bit into his sandwich, watching Ben Johnson. But Robey felt his skin crawl and looked again. The police car no longer rested at the place it parked. Robey turned completely around and after a few seconds saw the police car slipping slowly along between rows of parked cars, now only three rows behind them.

He reached out with his left hand and shoved Steve. "We may have problems. Get ready."

"Wha—?"

"Here, take the shotgun. . . . Here's more ammo." Robey leaned over the back of the front seat and picked up the AR-15 automatic rifle, smacked the clip sharply on the bottom, checked it, ready.

The police car continued its slow cruise, and Robey tried convincing himself the cops could be looking for anything —kids drinking beer or screwing, marijuana smokers, a stolen heap, runaways, anything. . . .

They could also be looking for a pair of bank robbers.

The police car rounded the last lane behind where Robey parked the Chevelle, passed along, then turned and came back in the lane which would bring them directly behind the Chevrolet.

At a distance of fifty feet, the police car abruptly stopped, and Robey knew then: this was it. . . .

Bellon drove and Stryker sat brooding when Patrol 21 came on the air, Elmore's calm, unemotional voice. Stryker reached for the microphone, but the frequency shrieked and howled with multiple transmissions. Like all police departments, this one had virtually no real radio discipline. Everyone wanted in on the act, if for no other reason than getting his name and/or car number on the tapes. The male police sergeant commanding the policewomen dispatchers' crew flipped his override switch and commanded, "Clear the air, clear the air. Patrol 21, repeat; Patrol Two-one, say again, say again."

Silence.

At the first transmission, Bellon swung the car around in a U-turn, jumping the concrete median, oil pan dragging and grinding, the transmission bumping hard, and traffic from the other direction jamming brakes, peeling rubber; but Stryker shouted, "CLEAR!" and Chino shot gas to the Ford. Stryker got on the radio, calling over and over, not waiting for acknowledgement, "Block the exit, block the exit, any car in vicinity block the exit."

Chino took the turn-in on two wheels and almost lost the Ford, slowed, jammed his foot down again. As they raced past the cashier's booth, Bellon and Stryker heard gunfire.

Neither Southwell or Elmore had any intention of approaching the suspect automobile. Neither man feared doing so; both feared wounding or killing innocents if this was *the* car and the shit hit the fan. They felt content, waiting for assistance; they had nothing to prove, nothing to gain and so much could be lost if they charged in rawjaw, gung-ho, John Wayne-ing it. They were professional police officers, lived by the creed and code:

Set it up so surrender is the only *intelligent choice.* . . .

But Southwell and Elmore did not know they had jammed up against a couple of trapped, frantic queers, one of whom went insane at the thought of capture, arrest, imprisonment.

Steve jumped out of the Chevelle, levelled the shotgun over the roof of the car, and fired. The charge blew a hole through the windshield between Elmore and Southwell. They dived out of the car, drawing their revolvers, crouching behind the car doors, returning fire.

Steve emptied the shotgun, then drew his revolver.

Almost with a sigh of resignation after cursing Steve and the boy's blind reaction, Robey turned on the hose, splatting three-round AR-15 bursts at the cops. He concentrated on the door nearest him first, pumping them in, three and three and three, and finally saw the cop sprawl on his back. He turned the AR-15 on the other door, fired a burst, then froze in amazement as the cop broke from cover and ran toward the Chevelle, dodging and crouching. Robey fired but missed, the bullets digging sprays of gravelly dirt and whining off into the night.

All around, people screamed and shouted and car lights came on. The magazine emptied, and Robey thumbed the catch and reloaded.

At that instant Robey heard three shots fired and in the

Micronite filter.
Mild, smooth taste.
For all the right reasons.
Kent.
KENT
America's quality cigarette.
King Size or Deluxe 100's.
ings: 17 mg. "tar,"
1 mg. nicotine;
00's: 19 mg. "tar,"
3 mg. nicotine
v. per cigarette,
Warning: The Surgeon General Has Determined That Cigarette Smoking Is Dangerous to Your Health.

Collect the Kent "Collectables."

Take advantage of this special Kent offer. Order these attractive items for your family and friends.

Please send me the following Kent Collectables:

- [ ] **A.** 4 qt. corn popper $9.95
- [ ] **B.** 30 cup insulated party perk $12.95
- [ ] **C.** 4 qt. insulated ice bucket $5.00
- [ ] **D.** 55 oz. beverage server $5.00
- [ ] **E.** Set of 4-16 oz. insulated steins $5.00
- [ ] **F.** Set of 4 insulated tumblers $2.50
- [ ] **G.** Set of 4-10 oz. insulated mugs $2.50

I am enclosing 10 Kent end flaps 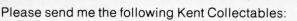 for each item ordered, plus check or money order. Offer continues as long as supply lasts. Allow 3 to 4 weeks delivery. I certify I am 21 years of age or over.

Name _____ Address _____

City _____ State _____ Zip _____

Mail to: Custom Service Co., P.O. Box 888, Maple Plain, Minnesota 55359

same instant heard the unmistakable, unforgettable sound of high-velocity slugs hitting human flesh. He spun around and saw Steve fall. He looked for the cop but could not see him. He jerked the handle and kicked the door open, ran around the car, and found Elmore crouched there reloading his revolver.

For a moment the men stared into each other's eyes, then Robey raised the automatic rifle and squeezed the trigger.

Bellon crammed the Ford's brakes and skidded sideways, stopping just inches behind the patrol car. He leapt out. drawing his revolver.

Stryker had his door open as they turned the corner into the lane, and before the car stopped he jumped, his Colt's Python in his huge left hand. As he charged past the rear end of the patrol car, he saw a man almost as large as himself throw open the back door of the brown car and leap out. an automatic rifle in his big hands. He recognized Robey at once. Stryker dropped to his right knee, drew the .357 Magnum up in a two-handed grip, and as Robey turned behind the car and faced Elmore, Stryker fired.

The slug hit Robey's spine, and his back arched as he squeezed the trigger, hand clamped in a death grip. The entire magazine ran off, some rounds into the air, the remainder into the ground, as Stryker fired again, once more, the .357 Magnums slamming into Robey like runaway trucks. knocking him end over end.

Stryker approached cautiously, gun ready. Elmore lay bleeding, shot in the left calf, the right thigh, and the lower belly, by Robey's last wild shots. He said nothing, made no sound.

Stryker stepped past Elmore and placed the muzzle of his Python against Robey's head, and waited. Robey did not move. Stryker held the gun in place, grabbed Robey's shoulder and jerked him over on his back. One look at the places where the Magnum slugs exited told Stryker that Robey was dead.

Chino's voice sounded as though it came from the bottom of a well. "This one's endgate, Col. Three in the 10-ring."

"Get an ambulance. Elmore's shot to pieces. See what Southwell looks like."

Then the drive-in filled with police cars . . . city, county, state, FBI.

Southwell was dead. Elmore lived after ten hours' surgery.

10—TAKING BOWS

The day following the gunfight FBI Special Agent In Charge H. Ardd Peters issued a statement to media:

> *Today the FBI announced the capture of Harmon Robinson and Stephen Rayne, wanted on federal warrents for unlawful flight to avoid apprehension and unlawful flight to avoid prosecution for the crimes of murder, bank robbery, armed robbery, felonious assault, and other charges. H. Ardd Peters, Special Agent In Charge of the local FBI Office, said that subjects Robinson and Rayne violently resisted arrest, and in the ensuing gunbattle both men died as a result of gunshot wounds inflicted by arresting officers.*
>
> *Subsequent investigation, SAIC Peters reported, reveals subjects Robinson and Rayne have been identified as the murderers of teenage Kelly Joe Cain during a bank robbery in Phoenix, Arizona, as well as perpetrators of similar crimes in Southern California and through-out the Southwest.*

The standardized FBI press release appeared without change in the *Tribune* and *Journal* and all on broadcast media hourly.

Elmore's survival earned a sidebar story, with God getting star billing, while none of the dedicated surgeons who worked ten hours saving Elmore was named.

Southwell's name appeared in the obits of both newspapers.

Stryker's name appeared in neither newspaper and was not mentioned on radio or television, nor was Bellon's.

Neither Bellon nor Stryker thought much about the press release. They certainly did not resent it. Both had been victims of such tactics on many occasions. They knew it was often standard procedure to issue releases contrived so that, without actually stating that a ranking officer made the arrests, solved the crimes, or had the gunfights, the readers, listeners, and viewers could hardly conclude otherwise.

Both Stryker and Bellon did make some snidely gross, obscene remarks to one another and fellow city cops and sheriff's deputies and state troopers about the several inaccuracies in SAIC Peters' canned propaganda.

Otherwise, Stryker and Bellon were far too busy searching for that goddam Mark IV and had no time for sweating small stuff.

Sam Borchia was sweating, learning how Arnold Witterstadt had felt. . . . There was no telling what kind of incriminating evidence might be in that goddam IV. And Sam did not need reminding nine times a goddam day by The Man in Phoenix how important it was Sam find the car before the cops did, though this did not stop The Man's insistent telephone calls.

Sam finally blew his cork: "Look, get the hell off my back, will-ya? I can't do both! Stay on the phone with you, and search for the car, too!"

The Man acted as though he had not heard Sam's outburst and applied more pressure. "I'm sending in some of my boys."

"I don't need your *boys!*" Sam shouted. "All they gonna do is draw attention, f' Crissake!"

Under the pressure Sam made a singular mistake; he went personally to The Sundowner and inquired about the Mark IV and Robey.

Carlosito insisted, "It was *him,* I'm telling you. I *saw* him, I asked the girl and she *told* me!"

Stryker and Bellon went out; they showed the girl six photos and asked her if any of the men had been in recently, making inquiries about the men who'd rented a room and registered as Robey. The woman thumbed through the photos, and the instant she spotted Sam, she said, "Him."

100

They took her downtown where she made a sworn statement which she signed.

They went back to their office and found Southerlund with his feet up, talking on the telephone. Stryker pushed the button down, and Southerlund dropped his feet to the floor.

"What are you doing here?"

"My three days are up."

"Three days?"

"DC Seamon gave me three days without pay for my foul-up, when that meskin called in."

"And that's it?" Bellon said, balling his fists. "You have nothing else to say about it?"

"Should I?"

"If you were a man you'd be biting a gun barrel," Chino snarled. "Southwell's dead and Elmore's dying because you doped off, you assfaced, shit-sorry, mother—"

"You're crazy. . . . Hey, skipper, get this guy off my back!"

"What guy? I didn't hear anything."

"Southerlund, I will cave in your fucking face if you're still here when I come back." Bellon wheeled around and went out the door.

Stryker said, "Zenner, you'd better go cool Chino down."

Zenner left and Stryker closed and locked the door behind him. He looked at Southerlund, gameface. Southerlund backed around so a desk came between him and Stryker. Stryker said nothing, he just stared at Southerlund, gameface. He watched fear come into the man's eyes, followed by defiance, then righteousness, then fear again.

Stryker said, "You got one of our men killed and another shot to pieces. What are you going to do about it?"

"You're crazy, that wasn't my fault."

"You're crazy if you've bullshitted yourself into believing it was *not* your fault." Stryker spat a long thin brown stream that struck Southerlund in the face. "I'm gonna dogchow your worthless ass, Southerlund, if you ever show your kisser in this building again. I'll pound you to a pulp, then drag you through a knothole dick first. I'll stomp a mudhole in your back, then double you over like a break-open shotgun and make you pee in the hole. Southerlund. I'll *kill* you, you ever come under my sights again! You dig, *Dick Tracy?*"

"Ye—Yea—Yes, *sir!*" Southerlund suddenly bent double and puked, spewing rotten slime down his front and covering his shoes.

"Seems you have it *on* with John The Baptist, so you see him about your next assignment."

Stryker unlocked the door and walked out. He went to the toilet, and when he came back only Southerlund's odor remained. Stryker picked up the phone and dialed. "Jail, Basen," a voice answered.

"Base, this is Stryker. Send a couple trusties up t' my office with a bucket and mops."

"You oughta quit tappin' so hard on those assholes, sarge."

"I wish I had tapped on the bastard."

"They be right up."

"Thanks."

While the jail trusties finished cleaning, Zenner and Bellon returned; they had cups of coffee and one for Stryker. Chino sniffed, then smiled. "You dump him, Col?"

"Never sweat small stuff. Let's get working. *Where* is that friggin Mark IV?"

"No parking ticket on either bod or in the Chevelle," Zenner said. "I *know* . . . because when I got the word from Auto Theft it was stolen, I dismantled the sumbitch, from headliner down."

"Which leaves us what?"

"Some third guy's got it."

"You believe that?"

"No way," Bellon answered. "Those assholes made a pair, no help wanted."

"They could have hired someone to drive it out of town," Zenner said, reaching.

"Zenn—"

"OK, OK. So?"

Stryker leaned across the desk facing Zenner and Bellon.

102

"You know what we *have?* A case on Borchia! . . . if we find the car. Borchia fingered the bank job. He *had* to meet those assholes, some time, some place. I'm betting Bella Napoli."

"Absolutely," Zenner said. "He's a showoff bigshot who'd never pass a chance like that, putting it on for out-of-towners."

"Let's roust his help," Chino said.

Zenner shook his head, sadly. "They'd never talk, the way Sam's got the hammer on them." He shook his head again. "They have their jobs to think about."

"Then burn the lousy place down," Chino said savagely.

Zenner actually stumbled backwards under the impact of the words and their portent. His mouth worked, and finally he managed to say, "You can't be serious!"

"Gimme a torch and I *show* you I'm serious or not!" He leaned toward Zenner. "Southwell is *dead,* man. You got a nice wife and four kids, and it could have been you, Zenn, *dead!*"

"But that's what separates us from the assholes, Chino. The rules."

"*Fuck* the goddam rules!" Bellon shouted and then began crying. He turned and walked away blindly and sat down facing the wall.

Stryker said quietly, "Southwell and Elmore broke Chino in when he came out of Academy, Zenn."

"Oh—"

"Hang in here a while with him till I get back."

"Sure, skip."

Stryker ignored the DC's policewoman secretary and went into Seamon's office. Without preamble, Stryker said, "I want an explanation."

"I beg your pardon!"

"I'd like to settle this here."

"You're required to make an appointment—"

"I'm running thin. If I leave here unanswered, you know where I'm going."

"Sit down."

"This won't take long. . . . I ran Southerlund up on a serious charge and could have proved criminal negligence if you had not short-stopped me."

"That was within my jurisdiction, as you well know, *sergeant.*"

"Are you *listening*? I said a *criminal* charge."

"It was my judgment——"

"Your *judgment*? Based upon *what*? I had not even filed a detailed report before you ran under me and slapped his wrist with three days."

"I am not obliged to check my decisions with you, Stryker!"

"You bloody well do with a higher authority, and I'm taking it up."

"Now, Colin, sit down and let's talk."

"Colin? A minute ago it was *sergeant,* in a loud voice."

"All I want is an explanation. Why do you feel so——so *dedicated* about pursuing this innocuous matter."

"Innocuous. . . ." Stryker grinned with his gameface on. "If I'm wrong, correct me; but innocuous means harmless, right? Harmless. We have a dead cop and another dying because Southerlund doped off."

Stryker moved against the desk and leaned over facing Seamon. "You guys humping the same puss?"

"WHAT?"

"DC, I've got a bulletin for you. You don't smoke, never drink, wouldn't say shit with a mouthful. You're the civil service commission's darling, ideal cop . . . except they don't know——and you think no one else knows——that you'd prong a goddam rattlesnake if someone held its head."

Seamon went white.

Stryker bore down. "Nora Bocanegra? Rosario Montelongo? Ruth Anderson? Edna Ludlow? You want more? A bunch, in twenty years! How about Billie Easom, that's Mrs. Patrolman Garland Easom?"

Seamon's voice sounded as though he spoke through sandy stones. "What do you want?"

"That lousy Fubar Southerlund fired."

104

"I can't. He's been punished, double jeopardy."

"DC, try your best, and I bet you'll come up with a way despite all obstacles."

"All right, I'll see—"

"I want the paper back."

"What paper?"

"DC. . . ?" Stryker gamefaced him. "Mrs. Sergeant Richard Cook?"

"What are you, a goddam internal security snitch?"

"Well, listen to that. John The Baptist using the Lord's name in vain!"

Seamon dug out the folder from his desk and handed it over. Stryker smiled. "You forgot to endorse it."

Seamon reached, but Stryker pulled the folder back. "Just a few kind words on a hunk of your official stationery will do fine, DC."

In his office, Stryker found Bellon smoothed out, drinking fresh coffee with Zenner. "Zenn," Stryker said, "hang in here on phone watch. While the FBI shuffles papers, clearing up those big unlawful flight warrants," he grinned, gameface, "and *solves* the bank robbery, and stands around taking bows, Chino and I are going out and follow up on the case."

"What do I say, in case someone calls for you?"

"Just that. Chino and I are on a follow-up. We are going to find that Mark IV, and we are going to tie it and those assholes to Sam Borchia who fingered this job."

Stryker threw the folder on the desk. "While you're resting, type this up clean, delete all Seamon's crappy revisions, and shoot it straight to the Super's office, authority John The Baptist." Stryker placed Seamon's endorsement atop the folder.

Stryker turned and smacked Bellon on the back, hard. "Come on, down-mouth. I'll buy *one* drink, then it's work, work, work. Forget your social life, all that strange puss you been cutting, work, work, work. Follow-up!"

11—FOLLOW-UP

In the car, Stryker repeated, "Keep thinking, getting your head on like Robey's. Where did you put the Four?"

"Think? I've been *dreaming* it, when you let me off five hours."

Stryker almost said, "If you don't like the game, hang up your jock," but stopped himself in time. Neither of them had gotten much sleep since the bank job went down, and Stryker figured his fuse had grown shorter than Chino's because Doris had been on him like stink on shit, the way she flared at him while he shaved that morning (after coming in at 3 a.m. and falling dead beside her, most of his clothes still on):

"If all you need is a place to flop, why not move to a damned motel? Your daughter's beginning to wonder who *is* that big grouchy man that comes around every few days?"

"OK, OK! Soon as we find that goddam car, I'll take some days off. We'll run up to Taos, cool off in the mountains."

"Oh, *sure!* Any time you get two days off you go to the mountains, all right, *alone!*"

"Let's not argue about my mother again, Dori. She's an old woman who's lost four sons and her husband. I live closer than Duncan or Brice, so I'm obliged to visit her when I can. Plus I *want* to visit her when I can."

"I still don't see why she refuses to move to town."

"If you'd ever bothered getting to know her, instead of characterizing her as 'quaint', like she's some kind of freak, maybe you'd know."

"I thought we weren't going to argue about her . . . again!"

"I said we'd go to Taos, Dori; now drop it."

"You want breakfast?"

"I don't have time."

"Yeah, sure, I understand."

"I wish the hell you did. I was a cop when we married, and you had plenty of warning. I must have called you and broke a hundred dates at the last minute, or just never showed up!"

"All right, all right. Maybe you can go on ten hours sleep a week, but I can't."

"So hit the sack."

"So I'm going."

Which had been a beautiful start. Stryker thought; and I'm about to claw my partner because I quarrelled with my wife. . . .

Bellon said, "I can't get away from a parking lot."

Stryker did not speak, knowing Bellon was not talking so much as thinking aloud, working his head around toward Robey's mind.

"I mean, where else? He left it on the street, any reasonable place, it would have been found by now, right? OK, there *are* places in this city, every city, where a car gets lost forever; but not a Mark IV. He tried parking that boat in a *barrio,* and it'd be stripped before he got around the corner."

"Or stolen!"

"That's what I'm saying. It's been a week and no sign, no hint. And the heat we've put on Patrol and Traffic, everyone, including ourselves—If that car was on the streets we'd have it by now."

"Probably."

"So what else can we eliminate?"

"Motel, hotel, café, bar, movie, such-like parking lots. It's automatic for patrolmen, all cops, to check out cars left past closing time at business places."

"So that leaves just two places I can think of. A private garage or storage place, or a regular parking lot."

"I don't go the private bit. Why complicate things? I mean, hell, a guy would *have* to wonder, right? Some classy dressed dude wanting to stash a Mark IV a few hours.

107

The guy's got to tell himself, 'Whoa, now, this dude's *wrong*,' and the last thing you could call Robey's stupid. Crazy, you frigging well know it; but not stupid."

"So he put the Four on a lot. Which one? I think we counted about a hundred in the phone book. *And!* No ticket stub."

"Maybe he made a deal."

"How so?"

"Man, parking lots are cash business! Like junk dealers, pawnshops, loan sharks, doctors, lawyers, and all else; you know as well as I do. They *like* guys who don't want ticket stubs or receipts and pay cash. They pocket the money, make no record, pay no income taxes. I'll bet half the by-the-month customer never *see* a stub. The owner and hired help know the steady customers and their cars, no need for a stub. No ticket, no money paid, so far as the taxman ever knows."

The same thought occurred to both men at the same time. The missing Mark IV had gotten into the news briefly, until Stryker managed to kill it. But that could have been enough. Bellon drove to the towed-vehicle compound, and they found the Mark IV under a three-day coat of dust.

They went into the office. A big bulldagger with trimmed hair and shaved neck, wearing a man's shirt and trousers and Wellington boots, stared at them with flaring nostrils, as though the dog dragged in something dead. Stryker flashed his badge and said, "We want to know about the Mark IV."

"You guys from Auto Theft?"

"You saw my identification. I'm a cop, so is he, now stop wasting our time and get it on."

Hatred shone like crackling sparks from the lesbian's eyes, but she went to a green metal file box and, after a few moments' search, came back with a card.

"You got a machine copier?" Stryker asked, taking the card.

"No, why?"

Stryker ignored her and handed the card to Chino, and without asking went to her desk and picked up the tele-

108

phone. He dialed Identification Division and asked for Lieutenant Detective Gonzalez. . . . "Stryker, loot. We found that Mark IV."

"No shit? Where?"

"Right under our dumbutt noses. At the towed-vehicle compound. We want the works on it, OK?"

"Damn right. I'll be out with the truck in fifteen minutes. I'll bring along those assholes' fingerprint cards, make comparisons right there."

"Gonzy, bring one other card, too, will you?"

"Name it."

Stryker turned toward the bulldagger. "Get out of here!"

She began a protest, did a doubletake on Stryker's game-face, and hurried out the door. Stryker told Gonzy: "Bring Sam Borchia's card."

"Hey! You think that slob's tied into this?"

"We'll know after your crew works the car over."

"Fifteen minutes."

Stryker called the clerk back. He put the card on the counter before her. "The duplicate on this car go in the same day?"

"Absolutely. Always. We can get an instant contract cancellation if we—"

"How?"

"The patrol district car comes by on the way in, between eleven-thirty and midnight and takes the day's cards—"

"That means *always* running a day behind, say a car was towed just after midnight?"

The clerk nodded, and shrugged. "It's ATB's system, not mine."

Chino said, "Auto Theft has no graveyard crew."

"Some fucking way to run a railroad!" Stryker said. "They start every morning a day behind. With a heavy workload, zap! Three days behind." He tapped the card. "How did this car come in?"

The bulldyke took the card and, after a glance, said, "The guy at the lot called it in, abandoned."

Stryker shoved the card to Chino. "Take a run over

there and see just what the hell's going on at that place. I'll hang in here for the ID crew."

Though Stryker found no fault whatever with the manner Lt/Det Gonzalez and crew attacked the job he felt his impatience becoming anger when each newly lifted latent print underwent comparison and was found to be Robey's or Ray's or some unknown person's; never Borchia's.

Then Det/3 Ellinger found the matchcover. He took it from under the seat-back on the driver's side, carefully, with tweezers. Stryker followed him into the mobile crime-lab van. The matchcover's outer side was glossy jet black, plain on the reverse side, with a BN in blood red lettering on the front, the B above the N, letters connected, in the fashion of a livestock brand.

Anyone who lived or passed through northern New Mexico and read newspapers, listened to radio, watched TV or saw billboards, recognized the Bella Napoli "brand."

Ellinger dusted the cover, found a beauty latent on the reverse side, photographed it, lifted it, made the comparison. He turned and grinned so widely Stryker thought Ellinger's face would crack. "Big Sam's left thumbprint."

"If you weren't so hairy, I'd kiss you!"

Ellinger blew a raspberry through his scraggly moustache.

Bellon returned a few minutes later with the kid from the parking lot, pimply, ratty hair, wiseass sneer twisting his lips. They walked him into the office, and Stryker gave the bulldyke the thumb. After she left, Bellon said, "OK, assface, let's have it from the top again . . . and this time just leave out all the *crap!*"

"Listen, I know my rights."

"You son of a bitch," Stryker said, gameface, "we've got a dead cop and another dying, killed by the bastards who owned that car out there. That goddam car stayed on your parking lot four frigging days, then all of a sudden someone gets spooked and calls it in abandoned. The only

110

rights you're going to get are your *last* fuckin rites if you don't start dropping your mud, *now!*"

The sharp shrewdy with the pimples and scummy hair told it fast and he told it right, blinking sweat from his eyes and wiping his salty lips.

"OK, that explains the lock combination we found on the punk," Bellon said.

"You toss the car?"

"I swiped the jack and spare and some clothes outta the trunk," and he suddenly looked away.

"OK, smartass, have it your way. Just don't say you weren't warned." Bellon spoke almost wearily, as though he had chores he disliked extremely. His big hands suddenly shot out faster than the kid could see. He got the kid's ears, twisted and lifted. The wiseass shot to his feet in an effort to relieve the up-pulling, twisting agony, both hands flying up, plucking at Chino's hands. Stryker pivoted on the ball of his right foot and sank his huge left fist into the skinny gut, feeling the spine against his knuckles.

The wiseass collapsed, unconscious, doubled and gagging, his legs pumping erratically as though he might be riding a bicycle, not too well. Stryker picked him up by the belt and collar and took him into the toilet just off the tiny office. He upended wiseass and stuck him head down in the commode, and Chino flushed it. Wiseass came to, spluttering, hacking, vomiting. Stryker dropped him, and gave him a few minutes to screw his head back on. Then Stryker jerked him to his feet, doubled his left fist and with a backhanded pop, tapped the wiseass in the ribs, hard.

"How about it, asshole? You feel like maintaining a little eye contact now? Feel like assisting the police with their inquiries, as they say in Scotland Yard? I'm a big dude and don't tire easily. I can tap on you all day."

"Wise up, wiseass," Chino said. "This is a murder investigation. And the dead guy was a cop."

"I got the rest of the stuff at my pad."

"Stuff?"

"A couple guns, some ammo, clothes, and jewelry. . . ."

111

He swallowed, and it seemed as large as Stryker's fist going down. "At least ten or twelve thousand dollars. . . ."

They took the wiseass home, had him sign a Consent To Search form, and tossed his pad. They recovered two large, expensive, handmade leather suitcases, suits, slacks, shirts, ties and socks and custom-lasted shoes, cufflinks and tie-bars and rings, all tremendously expensive; two revolvers, two boxes of handloaded ammunition . . . and almost $15,000 cash. They booked wiseass and the evidence and rounded up some help.

Stryker and Bellon came down on Bella Napoli as it opened for trade at six that evening. They hit with six other detectives. Sam was not there. All the cops had eight mug-shots apiece. They isolated the personnel so they could not talk amongst themselves and interviewed each individually: the cashier, the maitre d', waiters, busboys and bartenders and waitresses, cooks, dishwashers, even the janitor.

Bellon cracked it.

Chino knew Sam would use the private dining room, so he learned the name of the waiter who customarily served Sam and smiled when Huero Garcia presented himself. Bellon and Garcia went all the way back together: born on the same block, attended the same school, got their first *pinoch* from the same giggly fat *puta*. Chino had also arrested Garcia on three occasions since becoming a cop; Stryker had dealt with Huero several times. Thus, Huero knew it would only be a matter of time until he copped anyway, because these *pinchi chotas,* friggin cops, would simply slap the shit out of him if he lied. Huero identified Robey and Ray as having dined with Mr. Borchia one evening about ten days ago. Huero got a $10 tip.

When the others who'd seen the gunmen learned Huero had dropped his mud, they came across, too, losing a job being nowhere as bad as sitting in jail; and all the cops kept impressing upon all the Bella Napoli hired help: this is a cop-killing investigation. They were all taken downtown to police headquarters where they gave voluntary, witnessed, notarized, signed statements, and were then released.

12—STRYKER'S FIRST WARNING

Donald Pickett had been an FBI Special Agent for thirteen years. the last nine in this particular office. He very much enjoyed being an FBI agent. He liked the prestige, the exceptional wages, the hours and fringe benefits, and the work for which he'd hired out. He did his work well and that fact plus his habitual good humor made him one of three agents in the city whom other cops trusted.

Pickett had actually been known to furnish information to other agencies from time to time. This was, of course, a direct violation of FBI rules, practices, procedures, and doctrine, which dictated The Bureau should *receive:* aid, assistance, unlimited cooperation, and complete access to the files, records, and information of other agencies.

But the FBI seldom reciprocated, except in ways which might work to the Bureau's advantage and/or come under the heading of propaganda and public relations. It was proud of its fingerprint files, its overrated crimelab (the crimelab operated by the Texas Department of Public Safety is superior; that in California almost equally good); the Bureau furnished guest lecturers, gave seminars on auto theft and tracing fugitives, and a few agents proficient in necessary skills taught courses loosely called "judo" but in actuality nothing more than a half-dozen basic holds, defenses. and falls.

The Bureau also gave guided tours of its offices and facilities in the larger resident agency offices. While conducting such a tour, two days after H. Ardd Peters assumed SAIC command. Pickett accidentally marred the bluing on the barrel of a .45 caliber Thompson submachine gun. This incident was reported by another agent, without Pickett's knowledge, such snitching off on fellow agents being not too unusual in certain law enforcement agencies.

Shortly thereafter, FBI Special Agent Donald Pickett received an official Letter of Reprimand for " . . . careless, abusive, irresponsible, and unprofessional handling of Bureau firearms."

Pickett's previous thirteen-year spotless record not withstanding, the letter automatically removed Pickett's name from any consideration whatever regarding promotion, choice assignments, increased responsibilities, possible transfer to the resident agency nearest his hometown, for which he had applied annually for the past four years. His father had died; his mother had become increasingly invalided, and he felt it his duty to be as near her as possible.

Despite all this, because of his natural and habitual good humor, Pickett could have easily endured such overkill for his miniscule violation of ". . . approved practices and procedures" . . . if SAIC had kept the trivial matter informal and inhouse.

But SAIC Peters so feared anything which might endanger his own position and record, he forwarded a full report to Washington. . . . So Pickett's letter hit like a thunderbolt, signed personally by The Director.

Even then, Pickett managed to ride with the punches, but Peters had not yet finished with him. Peters chose to regard Pickett's natural good spirits as an expression of insolent indifference toward his punishment. Peters transferred Pickett from his job as senior agent, major felonies and made him a "road" agent.

The job of road agent was a known dead-end assignment without hope for promotion or even eventual reassignment. It marked a man. It ranked among the worst fates which could befall an agent, with one exception, transfer to Butte, Montana, the acknowledged FBI equivalent of the Siberian saltmines. No agent ever left Butte, unless he resigned, retired, or died.

A road agent spent Monday through Thursday "on the road" every week. He checked with local officers in the tiny towns and villages within the home office's jurisdiction. He had coffee with a constable in this village, with the sheriff in that county seat, the chief of a three-man police

114

department in another town. The road agent spent all day Friday in his home office dictating a complete report of his activities while on the road Monday through Thursday. He spent the weekend with his family, unless called out for extra duty.

Peters told Pickett when he notified him of the transfer, "Your name is at the top of the extra-duty roster, and it will remain there so long as I'm SAIC of this office." He took off his glasses and wiped the corners of his eyes. "If you don't like it, resign."

That was the only choice Pickett had: FBI agents have few rights, no ways or means for appealing to higher authority when they believe they have been treated unjustly. There is no civil service commission or other authority available, including the courts. Officially, The Bureau denies that it requires agents to sign a resignation before it appoints them to office, but *no* agent has ever in the Bureau's history successfully challenged any assignment, reassignment, transfer, reprimand, suspension, or dismissal.

It was from this background and knowledge that Donald Pickett found sufficient motive to call Stryker and tell him:

"Colin, watch your ass. Peters will cram you if he gets the chance. He's running a background on you because you made a fool of him that night at the bank."

"Don, why are you telling me this?"

Pickett told Stryker what Peters had done to him personally.

"He'll try and down you on civil rights if he gets a beef from anyone at Bella Napoli. He'd damned well initiate a case if he can make it stick."

"What's his problem?"

"He's just a ruthless son of a bitch, right out of the Jesus Edgar mold. You offended him. So he'll stomp your meat off, give him the chance.

"OK, Don; thanks for the warning."

"Something else, too."

"Yeah?"

"Tell Ruebaugh our guys shook that bank guard's pad and came up with dozens of pawn tickets and some funny receipts. My guess, a shylock had Witterstadt by the throat and conned him into setting up the bank. They blew him up so he couldn't crack open under interrogation. . . . You know by now, I suppose, the back door was unlocked and the alarm system turned off?"

"Fits together nicely."

"It does that. Tell Clyde those pawn tickets all came from Central Avenue Loans."

"Fess Waxmann."

"We've got a raw data file on him reads like a wild-west novel; receiving, concealing, passing stolen government property and thefts from interstate shipments, dealing drugs and smuggling wet Mexicans, you name it. He's been nailed once on a chickenshit government check conspiracy case, plea bargained and copped for misdemeanor, did four months in La Tuna, the rest on PR parole."

"Why are your guys sitting on those pawn tickets?"

"You know that glory-grabbing bastard Peters. He wants a big case on the bank job, tying in Waxmann and Borchia and anyone else he can. The only thing is, he's shit on everyone since the day he got here. Our snitches have the word. We can't get enough piss to take aspirin with from them. They're spooked Peters will put them on the stand, break their covers, get them dogchowed . . . and if he'll treat an agent, one of his own men, the way he's treated me and a couple others, he'd help dig an informer's grave if it made the case so he looked good in D.C."

"Jesus."

"Colin, I, ah, well—I don't know you all that well. I mean, I know you are straight-arrow on the job . . . but if you have anything going on the side, a gal, like that, you'd better start using a pay phone."

"You means that son of a bitch is tapping in on me?"

"Not yet."

"Man, I can't believe this. I mean, I know you guys take a lot, and this credit grabbing bullshit, 'adopting' cases other cops make for you; but this's un-friggin-real!"

"He wants your ass so bad his eyes cross when someone

116

mentions your name. What the hell did you *say* out at the bank that night?"

"Hell, Don, I don't even remember. He came on strong, the bigshot bullshit, and I popped off. Right after that the gunfight went down. No lie, I don't have the vaguest notion what I mouthed off at him."

"OK, I've been on too long as it is. Just remember what I said."

"You sticking in?"

"You kidding? Thirteen years on the job, making better'n twenty grand a year. No way I could match that even if I had another trade, like plumbing or welding. I don't have any choice but stick in."

"Well . . . *tenga suerte, amigo,* have luck, pal. I hope it's not too lonesome out there on the road."

"Make it standing on my head. And you keep your ass covered, hear?" Pickett hung up.

Stryker told his wife, "I've gotta see a guy; be back in about an hour."

"Colin! You promised!"

"I'll keep my promise! Tomorrow! The promise was for tomorrow, Dori."

"Unless you stay out all night working again and don't feel like—"

"We're going, we're going. I won't be out all night. I'll be back in an hour."

He drove to Lt/Det Clyde Ruebaugh's house. Ruebaugh commanded Robbery-Homicide Squad. Stryker told him about the pawn tickets.

"Those sons of bitches," Ruebaugh swore. "When we tossed Witterstadt's pad I *knew* someone had been in ahead of us and I asked that bastard Ellis if they took anything. 'Not a thing, Clyde,' the lying little shit told me!" Ruebaugh bit through his wet cigar. "The thing is, I can't do anything about it. I can't go running to my man, 'Hey, Chief, those friggin agents took some evidence from Witterstadt's pad, would you please call their boss and get it back for me?'"

"But knowing is better than not knowing."

117

"Shit-I-reckon, tying Waxmann in, which ties in Borchia. God, I'd love to down that slob!"

"Wouldn't we all?"

"Anybody seen him since you got statement from those Bella Napoli people?"

"Not that I've heard."

"You guys got a surveillance on his house?"

"I don't have men for that."

"Nor I. We've got some snitches checking around, but no kickback from them."

"Sam's watering at night, but he's still around. He's got too much action going, and since we dogchowed Ruga, Sam's got no right arm he can leave things with, safely."

"You still feel we don't have enough for a warrant?"

"Not the way things are today. Ten years ago, we'd already have Sam in front of a jury. Waxmann, too. But I know our DA would never take the case, even if we got a warrant for Sam and Wax from our tame jaypee."

"Yeah, he don't like tough ones, that DA. Especially since this's election year and he's running hard."

"For governor."

"I figure so, after another term as DA." Ruebaugh put a fresh cigar in his mouth and rolled it side to side till it became slobbery with spit. "You're right. He'd never take the case if we presented it to him, so it's best we let Sam soak a while, let him sweat, wondering how much we know. Makes it tougher for him to line out a defense, get his witnesses bought, you know. . . ."

Stryker got to his feet and stretched. "Well, watch out you don't get mugged, Clyde; and I'll see you in a couple days. I'm taking Doris to the mountains tomorrow and see if we can get acquainted again."

Ruebaugh laughed and waved and Stryker stepped off the front porch and went to his car.

118

13—SAPPER

Stryker's comment to Clyde Ruebaugh had been entirely correct: Sam Borchia had not left the city, and he watered at night—a cattle-country expression which meant keeping a low profile, staying hidden from men you owed money to or who might otherwise have reason for finding you.

But while Sam watered at night, he did not sit on his hands and wait for lightning or the law to strike him dead.

Through his own informants, particularly a bent vice squad plainclothesman, Sam knew almost as much about the progress of the bank job investigation as did Stryker, Ruebaugh, and the FBI.

The more he cranked over his problems in his mind, the more enraged Sam became: two sons of bitches, Stryker and Bellon, lay at the center of all his troubles. Mainly Stryker. . . . OK, Bellon had his own balls, and enough guts to fill a butchershop, but he worked for Stryker; and Stryker kept after the case, grinding on it, keeping it alive, while that arrogant new FBI turd strutted around before the TV cameras: "Case closed!"

Stryker!

Sam felt the walls pressing against his fleshy body, but he kept himself under control this time. No crazy threatening phone calls, no shooting from the hip. He made himself think about his position for three days, and he kept arriving at the same conclusion. Stryker had to be whacked out.

Sam looked at his wristwatch, then he slipped out of the TV "Star's" apartment with six rolls of quarters in his pocket and went to the phone booth in which he'd already broken the light so he could talk at night without advertising his presence. He got the operator and placed a station-to-station call to a number in Chicago, Illinois. After the third ring a gruff voice answered, "Yeah?"

119

"Let me speak to New Mexico Sam."

"He ain't here."

"I'll leave my number?"

"Shoot."

Sam repeated the number on the pay phone dial.

"I got it down. It may be a while."

"I'll wait thirty minutes. If he don't call, I'll be back at this number two hours from now and wait again."

"Check." The line went dead and Sam hung up. He got out of the booth and stood in the shadows of the building, but still close enough so he could easily hear the phone ring. Exactly twenty-six minutes later it rang. Sam jumped half outside his skin, then walked fast and answered.

"New Mexico Sam says you should call at this number," and the same voice as before read it off, then hung up.

Sam got the operator again and placed another station-to-station call, feeding in quarters. The phone on the other end lifted at first ring. "Go ahead."

"Kell?"

"Big Sam?"

"Right on."

"Long time."

"You know it, babe. You OK?"

"Pretty warm down here."

"I heard."

"Can we do a little business?"

"Why not?"

"Because it's a very heavy, Sapper."

"A cop, huh?"

"That's right."

"If it suits you, Sammy, it's fine with me."

"This is no ordinary cop, Sapper."

"We've got a few total-tough sumbitches around Chi, too. I never saw a cop I can't whack."

"I just wanted you to know I'm not pulling anything that you should find out after you get here."

"I don't think you'd try screwing me, Sammy."

"When can you get here?"

"Speak to me of green, Sammy?"

"Five grand."

"It's been nice talking with you, Sammy; call any time you feel like chatting."

"I can go seven, Sapper; cash in front. But I'm—"

"No sad songs, Sammy, says Sapper." Kell laughed. Then his voice became icy, totally without emotion, and final. "Local or a fed?"

"City detective."

"How you want it?"

"Fast."

"No matter how?"

"I'm not interested in any trick shit, making it look like an accident or heart attack, that stuff. I want the bastard blown up, and your bottom price."

"Ten and expenses."

"That's *bottom?*"

"Take it off your fuckin taxes! You want him hit, it cost ten grand and expenses. Shit or get off the pot, Sam."

"Sold. When can you be here?"

"Next flight out. . . . And, Sam, no bullshit about the dough. Ten Gs in nothing larger than a fifty, no new bills, no consecutive numbers, you know how it goes. . . . And, Sam—the stories you've heard are true: fuck over me on the dough and I'll do a job on you, free of charge." Sapper Kell hung up.

When Kell got off the plane, he heard the public address speaker paging Mr. Cellars, one of numerous aliases Kell had used over the years. He stopped at the information desk, and the woman with an inch of pancake on her face handed him an envelope. Kell thanked her, went into the toilet, and entered a pay booth. He sat down and opened the envelope and took out $300 in $20 bills and a slip of paper with a telephone number on it. He memorized the number, balled it, shredded the envelope, put the money in his pocket and flushed the paper bits. He went out and collected his baggage and climbed into the Hilton Inn van. At the Hilton he went inside and called from a pay phone.

"Made it OK, huh," Sam said. "no problems?"

"Forget the small talk, Sam. Let's get on with the job. I want a vacation; it won't be here. How the hell does a lard-bucket like you stand this heat?"

"That's enough from you, too. I need to know, are you hot?"

"No way, no place, why?"

"I'm under surveillance, so—"

"So we don't meet."

"How about the dough?"

"Trust your faithful postman, Sam. You must be half outta your skull with your head on backwards."

"OK, you're right. Where'll I mail it?"

"I'm calling from the Hilton Inn. I'll take a room here, register as Jess Cellars, St. Louis, representing, ah, how about Salvage-Master, Inc.? I'm pulling your ass out of deep water, huh, Sammy?"

"OK, I got that. Now, the guy you hit is Sergeant Detective Colin MacGregor Stryker." Borchia gave Kell a description of Stryker and Stryker's home address. "If you need anything, I've got some guaranteed-cold tools."

"No, but thanks."

"How the hell did you get on the plane with anything, the security nowadays?"

"They don't search checked baggage, Sam. I think you've been out in the sun too much."

"When will you do it?"

"You're sure? How it goes down? You don't care how messy?"

"Just blow the sumbitch up, Sapper. Last week wouldn't of been soon enough!"

"I'll do just that, Sam. When I get the money."

Kell hung up, registered, went to his room, tipped the bellhop, got room service on the phone, and ordered a bottle of Scotch, ice, fresh limes, and club soda. He turned on the television and stripped off his sweaty coat, tie, and shirt. When the bellhop came with the whisky, Kell paid him in cash and tipped just right. He made a drink, then got the telephone book and opened it to the city map, on the blue pages between the whites and yellows. He found where Stryker lived, related it to the Hilton, and called down to the car rental desk.

Sapper drove the rental Plymouth out Central toward the university, then turned south on San Mateo. Ten minutes later, he drove past Stryker's home. He smiled, seeing a four-year-old Ford sitting in the open carport. The hit couldn't be much easier if this Stryker creep knew about it and cooperated in his own destruction.

Sapper made one more pass, then scouted the neighborhood. He decided he must stick with his first decision, made in Chicago. He did not know this city, and since Sam had not insisted upon finesse, Sapper would stay with his speciality, which had earned him a reputation and nickname: explosives!

He went back to the Hilton. He mixed a drink and chose one of his two matching expensive suitcases. He put the bag on the bed, unlocked and opened it. Inside lay another case, metal and of special design and construction. Sapper took the metal case out, then took a keylike device from his pocket which he inserted in an opening beside the case's handle. With extreme care, Sapper twisted the key as he bent over with his ear beside the opening. At the first tiny sound, he removed the key.

The atmospheric pressure in northern New Mexico differed from that in Chicago where Sapper had packed and then closed and sealed the airtight case, so he gave the pressure two full minutes to equalize slowly. He finished his drink and unlocked the case, took a long, flat bar from his other suitcase, and with the bar prized up the locking levers on the metal case, then opened it. To an uninformed observer, the case appeared empty. Sapper used the beveled end of the flat bar and sliced a straight line across the bottom lining. The bladelike beveled end went more than an inch deep. He made a parallel cut, then one across each end, then lifted out a strip sixteen inches long, three inches

123

wide, and almost two inches thick. What had appeared to be a smooth tan plastic lining inside the case was actually plastique explosive. From the foam rubber underside of the lid Sapper removed a fitted long flat box made of wood. He opened it, and inside lay a variety of mercury fulminate detonators—blasting caps wrapped in cotton on foam rubber padding. For these the case had been made. The deadly caps were so extremely sensitive that sudden changes in atmospheric pressure or temperature, or shock, could detonate them. Before the extreme security measures went into effect at airports, Sapper had carried the caps on his person; but he could no longer do so without risking detection. It had taken months and great expense to design, build, and test the case. He carried the plastique in the same case because it was convenient though incredibly dangerous— packing detonators with explosives, something no informed amateur would ever do; but Sapper had found an easy, though somewhat expensive, way to avoid any personal risk. He brought two airline tickets, under different names, sent the suitcase with the tools on one flight and "missed" the plane; then took the next plane using the other ticket. If the case full of plastique did go and drop an airliner out of the sky, tough shit; he wouldn't be on it. The same with rough handling: the baggage smashers would smash no more. Frig'm!

In the other suitcase, with his clothing, Sapper had a disassembled sawed-off shotgun, a silencer-equipped handgun, and ammunition for backup. Sam OK'd dirty and crude, so if the set looked right, Sapper would bomb the cop; if not, he'd pull up beside him at a traffic stop, shove the shotgun in his face and let it off or pop him with the hand gun when he answered the door. The guns were last resorts, though, in a town he did not know. It took too much time, wasted his money, figuring routes and plans and contingencies, clamping a tail on the guy for a week or ten days to learn where and when it was best to hit him. Sapper didn't do those jobs for any measly 10G.

Kell called room service and ordered an early dinner.

After eating and clearing all the dishes from the room. Sapper mixed another drink, undressed, and went to bed. He finished the drink, set his travel clock alarm for 2:00 the following morning, and promptly fell asleep.

Though Stryker left Clyde Ruebaugh's house with best intentions, he did not go straight home. He dragged Central, not really quite sure what he sought. He noticed Fess Waxmann's place had a dusty, deserted look, as though Central Avenue Loans had gone out of business but hadn't yet sold off its inventory.

Stryker circled the block, made a pass through the alley behind Waxmann's store, finding nothing. He felt a nagging uncertainty itching the back of his mind but found no remedy for it. Finally, chastising himself for wasting time he could use sleeping, Stryker headed home.

A few blocks from his house, Stryker passed a drive-in, quick-service, astonished at finding it closed. He looked at his wristwatch and could hardly believe he'd screwed away almost four hours!

Christ! Now he'd dick away a good half hour next morning filling the car with gas, buying ice and beer he could get so much cheaper in the city than on the road or in the mountains.

Stryker could already hear Dori's remarks about the delay next morning. His eyes felt grainy, and he suddenly yawned hugely, cramping his jaws, squeezing tears from his eyes. Christ, he needed sleep; a week of sleep. Once they got out of the city in the morning, he'd con Dori into driving. . . .

Stryker turned into his street off San Mateo. He spotted something wrong as he slowed, nearing his driveway. His cop mind and experience and finely honed skills that come only from self-discipline and practice—all alerted him to something not quite right; but he could not determine what it was. . . .

He drove on past his house, situated about mid-block,

and another block on farther, then turned south and snapped off his lights and stopped the car by shifting into neutral and using the handbrake, so his brake lights would not flash. He slipped the car into reverse and slowly eased back into the intersection and looked back along the street toward his home.

He saw nothing. But he felt it. With the handbrake, he stopped the car, shifted into low, cramped the wheels, turned and rolled forward, back along his street, lights out. With his left hand, he shifted his off-duty Colt's Detective Special forward and unsnapped the safety strap, hiking his tail-out shirt up and stuffing it inside his waistband out of the way. He coasted to a halt a block from his home, watched and waited. Nothing moved. He had just decided to disconnect the interior light, get out of his car and walk the street, when he grinned and sighed, knowing what he'd seen that was out of place.

A strange car stood parked at the curb in front of the Waylons across the street and a house west of his home. Stryker slipped the car into gear and switched his lights on, drove home. As he pulled into the driveway, he looked at the strange car, and he felt the wrongness again. A rental. . .?

He parked under the open carport, got out and locked the car after getting his flashlight from the glovebox, then walked across the street, revolver in hand, and checked the car. It was a rental, the small decal in a bottom corner of the rear window, four-door, dark green, blackwall tires, empty, locked all around. He stood for a moment, considered waking the Waylon family and asking them about the car . . . out of town visitors? Christ, though, almost 3 a.m. Stryker looked at the license number again, then walked back across the street and unlocked his back door and went into his house. He turned on the light over the stove and opened the refrigerator, hoping he remembered correctly and there was at least one Michelob left. He remembered wrong. There were two. He grinned and uncapped the first as he unbuckled his belt and slipped his holster and revolver off. He put them on the kitchen table and slacked into a chair, drinking deeply, sighing. Dori came into the kitchen wearing a shorty nightie. "Colin, did something happen?"

"I'm sorry I was gone so long, but nothing's wrong."

"We're still going?"

"You damn betcha!" He reached and she came and sat on his lap, and in seconds, it seemed, he was free of his trousers and she straddled him and the chair and he slipped inside the hot and wet. He placed his left arm under her buttocks and his right arm around her back, and she put both arms around his neck; then he rose, and without parting, with Dori keening in his ear, he carried her into the bedroom, bumped the door shut, moved his hand enough to punch the button, then laid her on the bed, never parting. . . .

Stryker took a shower and drank the second beer and they made love again. He remembered before falling into satiated, almost drugged sleep, something about that rental still bothered him.

When the alarm rang, Kell came instantly awake and snapped it off. He rose and dressed in dark jeans, light-weight long-sleeved turtleneck black jersey and a pair of black racers—low-quarter, soft-soled track shoes. He slipped on a red nylon windbreaker and stuffed a black stocking cap in the pocket. He checked the metal case: plastique, electric blasting caps, the handgun equipped with a silencer. He reached for the greener—the sawed-off shotgun—then changed his mind. From his other suitcase he took a wig and put it on, then a pair of thick-framed glasses with clear lenses. He left his room and went directly to his car, unworried about being seen. The red jacket kept him from looking like a burglar, the wig and glasses effectively disguised his real appearance so a make couldn't be put on him in a hundred years by an experienced cop.

He drove east out Lomas and turned south on Girard, worked back east on Central, south on San Mateo. He made a pass, astonished upon finding Stryker's car gone. He thought about going to the police station in case Stryker had been called out, or back to the quick-service market nearby and calling his home. Unawares, Stryker's wife would likely say where he'd gone. Kell made the block and stopped. Just then a car turned onto the street behind Kell. He flattened in the seat, then raised just enough so he could look between the top of the seat and bottom of the headrest which concealed the top of his head. He saw the car slow as though about to turn in, then continue on down the street. Kell recognized Stryker and his car. He also recognized what had happened, and his respect for Stryker jumped upwards instantly. A fast, quick, cool dude who knew what cars belonged on his street. Kell now appreciated Sam Borchia's concern and warning: "This ain't just any hick town cop."

Keeping his head low, still concealed by the headrest, Kell watched Stryker drive on down the street, at the second intersection make a right turn.

Kell knew what would happen then. In an instant, he grabbed his case and went out of the car, locking the door behind him. He ran lightly and fast across the street, up the driveway of the house next door to Stryker's home. He stopped between the side of the house and the car in the driveway. He sat down with his back against the wall an waited. A few minutes later, Kell saw a car without lights creeping forward—.

Kell opened the case and took out the handgun with the silencer, checked it for ready, silencer tightly screwed in place . . . and wished he'd brought the greener. But this could go down easy, no fret, no sweat.

Then Kell wondered—what the hell? Stryker suddenly turned on his lights and drove toward him into the driveway and parked. The lights screwed Kell. He had to move back deeper into the shadows, crouched low between car and wall. When he heard the car door slam and keys jingling, he raised up, but the light was much too bad and the range too great. Silenced firearms, despite movies and TV, had erratic range and accuracy. Before Kell quite realized what Stryker intended, the big man moved down his driveway and across the street and began checking Kell's car.

Kell braced his left shoulder against the wall of the house, knees up, elbows locked, two-hand grip, sighting on Stryker as he walked around the rental. Range and light worse than ever.

Kell kept being surprised and caught off guard by Stryker's speed and agility. One second Stryker stood looking over the rental and the next he'd jogged back to the dark shadows of his carport and gone in his back door. A dim light came on, then a brighter flash which went out almost instantly.

Kell sighed, but he spent no thought on missed chances. His business consisted of making absolutely sure. That's what his reputation and name were based upon, why he never negotiated fees, but only named a base price plus expenses and told potential clients to stuff it up if they could not pay that price. Since military service in Korea, Sapper Kell had earned over a million tax-free dollars killing people, sixty so far. Back home in his upper middle-class Chicago neighborhood, Kell owned a gift shop—through which also passed a great deal of stolen, smuggled, and otherwise "hot" artistic treasures.

He waited an hour, saw the bathroom light come on for twenty minutes, then go out; a few moments later the quick flash of light in the kitchen, which he'd figured now—refrigerator. Kell waited another thirty minutes, then he crept across the open space between the carports, slipped the catch, and raised the hood of Stryker's car. Working by feel alone, it took him less than ninety seconds to plant the charge, molding the plastique around the steering column tightly, inserting the electric detonator, wiring it to the nearest spark plug. He lowered the hood, slipped the latch, pushed the hood on down, released the latch, locked the hood in place. He faded through the shadows back across to the other house and waited five minutes. He'd waked no one. He moved out, light-footed, quick, along the fronts of the houses to the end of the block, then crossed the street and walked back to his car, got in and drove away.

Colleen Stryker woke at 6 a.m. She lay in bed a few minutes yawning and playing with her toes. Then she climbed off her full-sized single bed and went into the bathroom, shoved her padded box over beside the sink, stepped up on it, took her washcloth with the bunny on it from her special low-set rack, turned on the water and wet the cloth, soaped it and washed her face and hands and arms up to the elbows. Then she rinsed the rag and took a corner of it and scrubbed her teeth and gums. Everything just as Gramaw Stryker had taught her when she stayed almost one whole summer, a l-o-n-g time ago, when she was only three years old! Humming softly, Colleen Stryker silently mouthed the words, in Gaelic, to a highland reel Gramaw had taught her. She pottied, rinsed her hands again, then went into the kitchen. She got a box of cereal from a low shelf and her own personal private bowl and spoon, poured, got milk from the refrigerator and added it, sat on the floor and ate breakfast. What she spilled, she cleaned up. Gramaw Stryker had been very firm about that, you must *be* clean and *leave* clean. She was so nice, even if she was so tall and angular and wore cowpuncher clothes and talked so funny. "Aye, nae doot ye'll be ain bonny lass, though large I fear. A pity ye have yer Dad's heavy bone, ye may be tall's me fore yer doon!" and she lived so far from town, over the roughest old roads, and Mom nearly always cried when she went, so usually just her and Dad went on the long trip to Gramaw's. Grandmother, of course, lived right here in town, in a wonderful big old house that smelled like mice and dust and cloying talcum powder. She liked Grandmother, too; they were just different, Gramaw and Grandmother. . . .

Colleen went out into the back yard and ran. When running bored her, she got on the swing set and rode the "horse" for a while. Then she went back inside, letting the door slam.

The slamming door woke Doris Stryker. She stretched lazily, naked, and looked at her husband. They had been married six years, and still she looked at him with wonder. Not his size. In college she'd dated several athletes considerably larger, three of whom still played in the NFL. In fact, when she thought about it, Colin most compared to her Uncle Stace, who was not much larger than she, but had such enormous presence and self-confidence he seemed invulnerable. Stomach cancer proved that untrue. And, of course, Colin's partner, Bellon. In fact, she felt a bit uneasy around Bellon. . . .

She got out of bed, put on a robe, and went into Colleen's room. The child lay on her bed, covered with a film of sweat, reading. "Hi, Mom!"

"Have a good play?"

"Great, Mom; it's cool this morning."

"I'm going to the store for beer and ice, and gas the car. Want to ride along?"

"Sure, Mom," Colleen said and jumped off the bed, ran to her closet, and pulled a sunsuit from the low hanger bar.

Colin Stryker woke when the explosion caved in the side of his house and knocked him out of bed.

15—RAMPAGE

Not for one instant did Stryker question or doubt what had happened, even as he lay half-stunned on his bedroom floor. He shook his head, jerked on a pair of trousers and ran.

Hardly anything at all remained of his wife. Horrified neighbors stood gawking, two women screeching hysterically.

Stryker found his daughter lying almost fifty feet away, covered with burns, naked, left arm broken, three visible compound fractures, her left foot hanging by shreds. He literally jerked a terrycloth robe off Mrs. Waylon, tied the belt tightly around Colleen's left thigh just above the knee, then wrapped her in the robe.

At that moment a patrol car came howling around the corner, closely followed by a fire truck. Stryker thrust his baby in the patrol car's window, and the officer riding shotgun took her and without a word the driver roared off toward the hospital.

Stryker and the firemen gathered all they could find of Doris. Her right arm and both legs had been blown off. Her arm at the shoulder, her left leg above the knee, right leg at mid-calf. Her charred hips and thighs lay in the front seat. Her middle had vanished. Her head and shoulders and breasts, still more or less intact, lay spilled out onto the trunklid, having been blown through the back window.

When the second police car arrived, Stryker radioed an all-points on the rental car. The Superintendent of Police showed up, and media photographed him with his arm around Stryker's waist—he was too short to hug Stryker's shoulders.

"Son," the Super said, "what can I do? Just name anything and it's yours."

"Put a guard on my house."

"Of course, of course, after an attempt on your life like this, absolutely."

"I mean so all my stuff won't get stolen," Stryker said. "I can't lock the place with that hole in the wall."

The Super cleared his throat.

Stryker turned away and climbed back through the hole and went into his bedroom. He showered, dressed, and armed himself. He tried his phone; it was dead, too. He went out and got into the Ford as Chino drove up. "Let's go!"

"Jeez, Colin, I—"

"No use talking, Chino; I'm still numb. Hospital first. While I'm with the doctors, keep on that car."

The chief surgeon believed he could save the foot . . . if he saved the child. Colleen had multiple skull fractures in addition to the other breaks and the burns, and she lay in massive shock. Since he could not help, Stryker left.

Bellon met him as Stryker came out of Emergency. "Got the car, but the guy's blown."

"Rental from the airport?"

"Brought from there to the Hilton."

"Anything on the guy?"

"Nothing usable. He used the name Cellars, hotel and car both. Zenn checked by phone, the address and company are phony, driver's license stolen a year ago." Chino paused and sighed. "Pulled the oldest gag in the world. Claimed he had a sprain, so both hotel and rental clerks filled in the forms."

"And he paid for everything with well-used tens and twenties."

"Yep."

"That says all I need to know."

"Huh?"

"A professional hitman. Sam called in a bomber."

"We've already got the artist at the hotel working on a drawing."

"I don't need a drawing. . . . Sam will tell me who the guy is."

134

"Except where's Sam?"

"I can find Sam, pard. There's no place Sam can hide so I can't find him."

"Let's go."

"No, no *us,* pard. Me."

"Like you said—*pard.*"

"Not on this, Chino. This is going to get rough. I'll be up past my ears in shit if I don't get fired. I won't sacrifice you."

Stryker dropped Bellon at the police station and ten minutes later took down the back door of Fess Waxmann's Central Avenue Loans. He found dust and rat turds and an empty safe . . . and a telephone number.

He called Chino at the office and gave him the number. Bellon checked the criss-cross telephone directory, read the subscriber's name and address. "You know her. On TV, with the big jugs, used to strip in Juárez, all those hi-class places."

"Sam sponsers her daily show, right?"

"Exactly. I'll meet you—"

"No, wait for my call, then come like a jet!"

The trouble with a bombing was you might not get the person you contracted to kill. Rarely, but flukes happened. That meant you either had to stick around and watch the right guy get blown up, or you had to stay long enough to confirm it.

Kell sat in the airport coffee shop eating breakfast with a transistor radio plugged into his ear; he heard the first news flash, and disappointing it was. Son of a bitch! he swore silently to himself. He'd missed, got the cop's wife and kid instead. He couldn't finish his meal. God-*damit!* Now he was really in for it. Sam would be pissed, the Nationals would be sore as hell, the frigging town woud swarm with cops till the thing cooled down, and in the meantime he had to hang around this busher, stinking, hot meskiny town till he could set Stryker up again and whack him out, no ifs, ands, buts, or maybes.

Sapper Kell guaranteed results. That's how he'd made

135

$1,000,000 plus tax-free the past twenty years. When old Sapper went after them, he brought them down, or full refund; and he'd never parted with a dime he'd been paid for a hit yet.

He finished his coffee and fished out a pocketful of change and then dropped it, scattering coins all over the counter and floor as the second news flash came.

The cops had the rental car, had lifted prints from it, and issued an international alarm for a subject using the alias Jess Cellars, described as. . . .

Kell sat frozen in his seat, oblivious. People all around him stared, fascinated, at the man with the hearing aid who seemed to be having some kind of seizure. . . . Then Kell lunged to his feet and ran out the door.

He had already bought tickets on two airlines, checking the bag with explosives on one, the suitcase with his clothing and weapons on the other. . . .

But he had used the name Cellars at both!

He had to recover those bags, *now!* He almost broke into a run. Behind him a voice commanded, "Hold it right there, mister!"

Kell kept walking.

"You there! Stop!" Running footsteps, people beginning to turn, stare. He felt a hand grip his arm.

Kell let himself be turned, and he faced the airport security guard. Now his fear had gone, as it always vanished when he faced the final moment of truth. In addition to his skill with weapons and explosives, which he used ruthlessly, without remorse, Kell held another major, distinct advantage over almost every man he ever went up against:

He could defeat almost any man, with a sudden, savage attack. Not because he was so adept at unarmed combat. He knew no karate, judo, kung fu or any of that shit. But Kell knew the simple, basic fact that the ordinary American male, including many cops, is not prepared for such an attack. They cannot react swiftly enough to evade injury. They cannot cope with excruciating sudden pain, like the heel of a hand driven savagely against the nose. Their eyes shoot full of tears, their guts flip-flop, their minds go numb, some even call for their mothers. They are not only totally incapable of fighting back, but will stay home sick in bed for a week afterwards.

Kell looked stupidly at the security guard. Behind him stood a woman. Kell saw the nametag on her dress. "You forgot to pay your check, mister."

Kell looked at her stupidly, then again at the guard. Then he smiled, tapped his chest, screwed the ear-jack into his ear again. "WHAT? MY HEARING AID—"

"YOU FORGOT TO PAY!"

The woman held a check toward him. Kell slapped his forehead, took the check, looked at it, gave her $5. "OK?"

The guard looked at the woman, she shrugged, the guard shrugged, Kell turned and walked away. He went into the gift shop and brought a pair of large, aviator style sunglasses, a golf cap, and a sports shirt with pseudo-Indian designs and short sleeves. He stripped off his tie and suit coat as he walked to the toilet, and inside he changed shirts. The loudspeaker paged him, paged him again. . . .

Smartass cops, betting a longshot, hoping I haven't heard the news yet. Kell kept the earpiece in place, the radio tuned; but he heard no further reports. Probably the cops had clamped a lid on. It had been outrageously stupid, that second broadcast, but Kell thanked the asshole who'd broken it and warned him. He kept edging along in front of the ticket counters, checking departure schedules. Then Kell saw security guards, uniformed city or state cops checking identification of each customer at every counter.

Kell went toward the departure gates, and around each he saw a noticeable lack of uniformed officers but guys so obviously cops they might as well have been in uniform.

He went back to the telephones and called the number he'd gotten upon first arriving. It rang a dozen times. Kell hung up and dialed again. It rang and rang and rang. . . .

As Kell gave up, a ring cut short, and a voice answered, "Yeah?"

"Sam?"

"Yeah."

Kell frowned. "You sound funny, you OK?"

"You stupid bastard, how'm I supposed to sound!"

"Don't give me any shit, Sam. You said you had some guaranteed-cold tools."

"Not a chance, you friggin idiot!"

Kell said coldly, "Sam, I don't think you quite get it. I won't go down alone. I can break loose from this if I've got the equipment, but without it, I can't. You understand?"

"You're crazy!"

"Where, Sam?"

"So snitch me off. I'm a man of respect in this town. Nobody'd believe a crazy like you."

"Sam, shut your fat mouth and *think*. Can you really convince yourself Sapper Kell would give a stupid lard-bucket ghinny an edge, that I'd go on a deal with a shit like you and not protect myself? It's on tape, Sam. If the fuzz gets me before I take your head off, the feds get the tapes."

"You rotten bastard!"

"Sam, you're digging a wide grave."

"You son of a *bitch!*"

"Don't get so deep in you can't pay out, Sam. I can take a lot of mouth and write it off when a man's crapping his pants scared, but don't shove too far."

"You're on your own, Kell. Tapes will hang *you* worse'n me."

"How long you think you'd live, Sammy, after I had my first visitor in jail? Think about what happened to the woman and kid, say I make bond?"

Kell heard Sam's heavy breathing on the line.

"OK, I got no choice. Where are you? I'll have you picked up."

"By the cops, after telling them I'm armed, so I get blown up?" Kell laughed brutally. "You pick me up, in person. . . . *Shut up!* . . . This is not negotiable, you chickenshit would-be bigshot. You-pick-me-up—*personally!* It's the only hope you've got . . . of living, even coming clean if we handle it right."

Kell knew that last tiny suggestion of hope, preceded by utter hopelessness and certain death, would bring Sam.

138

Sam worked out the details and Kell agreed and they hung up.

Just as Stryker stepped off the elevator, he saw the door with 6D in brass at the end of the hall open. His hand flashed out and caught the elevator door, the bumper mushed back and the closing doors opened again. Stryker stepped into the car, let the doors close, and flicked the STOP switch. Moments later the buzzer in the elevator sounded and the 6 lighted. Stryker flipped the STOP button off and flattened against the wall.

The doors mushed open and Sam stepped forward. He saw a huge shape to his left and gasped, then tried to turn away.

Stryker hit Borchia just below the ear and Sam dropped like he'd been shot through the heart. Stryker dug his hand under Sam's belt and dragged him along the hallway. At the door of 6D, he searched Sam's pockets and found the right key, eased it into the lock and turned it gently, felt the bolt slide back. He drew his Python and slammed the door open.

The woman stood naked except for a bikini bottom, mouth round with silent scream. "Not a sound," Stryker said. She nodded dumbly, eyes bulging. Stryker dragged Sam inside, removed the keys, kicked the door shut. He dragged Sam on into the living room. A low divider separated the big room from the kitchen area. Stryker waved the revolver. "Get some ice and a wet towel."

The woman nodded. As she moved to the refrigerator, Stryker went like a cat into the bedroom, searched the closet, the bath, under the bed, and came back before she had the icetray emptied. "Move it!" Stryker commanded, "I'm in a hurry."

The ex-stripper had gotten her breath and some nerve back. "What the hell are you doing here, what do you want?"

"A little talk with Sam . . . bring the stuff!"

She came toward him, exaggerating the sling of her ass side to side, arching her back, her vast football-shaped bos-

139

oms jiggling and swaying. She tried a hesitant smile, but one look at the big bastard's face and she cut the act and thrust the baggie full of ice and the wet towel at him.

"Over here," Stryker said.

To her astonishment, Stryker gathered a fistful of Sam's shirtfront and jerked him to a sitting position, caught Sam under the arms and lifted him into Sam's favorite recliner chair. She knew Sam weighed 318 pounds. The big bastard cop didn't even pant. He motioned her around behind the chair. "Rub the back of his neck with the ice."

"Let me get some clothes on."

Stryker looked at her, stepped forward and slapped her. She went sideways ten feet, airborne. Her vision dimmed with stars shooting across the blackness behind her eyes. She felt herself jerked upright by her hair, held there by the aching, stinging strain on her scalp until her wobbly knees found strength and she stood. Just as she got her wind and the throbbing pain along the left side of her face began occupying her mind, her head jerked back and she stared at the pebble plaster on the ceiling. She tried twisting away and the grip in her hair tightened, and then Stryker slapped her across the back-arched taut belly, and she cried out. It felt as though he'd laid a branding iron to her flesh.

"No, oh, NOOOoooo," she whimpered.

"Good," Stryker said, "I don't like it either, roughing a woman." He turned loose his grip wound in her long dark hair and shoved. She stumbled across the room and fell in Sam's lap.

"Up!" Stryker commanded and she shot to her feet, almost as though coming to attention. "Use that ice on the back of his neck." Before she could move, Stryker slapped her with the end of the heavy, wet towel, and fire shot across her right breast. She squealed and sprawled as she reached for the ice baggie, got it, and scrambled to her feet. She tilted Sam's head forward and began rubbing his neck with the ice.

Stryker went to work on Sam's face with the towel, *splat —splat—splat*—back and forth, one side, then the other. Stryker stopped a moment, reached down and ripped Sam's

140

shirt from his body; his lardy breasts looked almost as large as the girl's. Stryker put the towel to him, *splat, smack, splat,* and Sam began moving, then moaning, finally crying out and jerking upright, eyes like platters.

Stryker dropped the towel and drew the Python and crammed the barrel between Sam's fat lips, shattering teeth. Sam reared back and the woman squealed. Stryker shot her a look. "Don't move. Keep the ice on him."

Stryker looked at Sam. "You hear me? Blink your eyes if you do."

Sam blinked. He tried leaning forward, making gagging sounds. "Swallow it, Sam," Stryker commanded. "Swallow it all, you rat-bastard shit." Stryker rammed the gunbarrel hard, feeling the high, ribbed front sight rip the roof of Sam's mouth, rammed till the cylinder rested against Sam's fat lips, four inches of cold steel gunbarrel gagging Sam, choking him, his eyes bulging. Stryker flashed his right hand up, open, and slammed Borchia across the ear. Sam bucked and Stryker rammed the gunbarrel in harder. He boxed Sam's ear again. The woman kept making tiny mewling sounds, like those of a kitten in pain.

Stryker cocked the revolver.

Sam shuddered, his eyes rolled up so Stryker saw only bloodshot whites, and Sam went limp. "No, no, Sam, none of that," Stryker said coldly, "no passing out. It's talking time, Sam," and Stryker slammed Borchia's ear again, and at the same time, holding his thumb on the hammer so the jerk would not fire the gun, Stryker ripped the Python's barrel from Sam's mouth and Sam fell forward, puking blood and bile and torn flesh and teeth chips into his lap.

"Talk to me now, Sam . . . or I'm going to kill you. . . . I'm going to beat you to death, slowly. . . . Sam, who bombed my wife and baby and where is the son of a bitch now?"

Stryker jerked Sam's head up and placed the revolver's muzzle between Sam's eyes. "Tell me, Sam."

Sam told him.

Stryker called Chino.

Stryker sat low, wearing a cap and sunglasses, behind the wheel of Sam's green Cadillac. He turned right off Girard, then 180 degrees back in front of the Skyport Terminal building. Kell walked briskly out the front door and opened the right front door of the car, ducked down to get in. He went sick and frozen in his guts when he saw Stryker. His muscles tightened to flee.

"Freeze, asshole, I'll gutshoot you. . . . Get in. Keep your hands on the dash, *up,* higher . . . scoot over closer." Stryker let his foot off the brake and jammed down on the accelerator, peeling rubber as he shot away from the terminal. The door slammed shut with the abrupt forward motion.

Stryker shot a look in the rearview mirror. Bellon and Zenner followed in a gray Ford, with Sam and the woman, now dressed, in the back seat, handcuffed.

"Kell," Stryker said, not recognizing his own voice, it sounded so dead, flat, cold, "I'm not going to tie you down. No handcuffs, nothing. Feel free to make a break any time you pump up your guts."

"And get shot in the back!"

"Jump out backwards, babykiller, if you've got a thing about getting shot in the back."

"You can't just kill me, Stryker."

"Why not? You *just* killed my wife and baby, trying to *just* kill me."

"Listen, I know my rights—"

Stryker held the Python wrapped in his left thumb and forefinger, the steering wheel with three fingers. He slammed the side of his doubled right fist into Kell's mouth, feeling teeth go. He struck again, splatting the nose. "Rights? Oh, you son of a bitch, tell me about your fucking *rights!*"

Stryker could not stand it any longer. He jammed the Caddy's brakes, driving Kell headlong into the windshield. Stryker rammed the shift lever into park. He dropped the Python down between the door and seat and spun with all his strength, driving the point of his elbow into the side of Kell's face as Kell slowly straightened from the shattered

142

windshield, crying with pain. Stryker shoved Kell over against the door, flipped the latch, and they spilled out on the pavement, rolling over twice, then Stryker came to his knees and pulled Kell up with him, measured him, gave him the best short chopping left uppercut he had. Kell's jaw shattered. Stryker lunged to his feet, keeping hold of Kell, and went to work on him with the left, pounding the liver, working on the ribs, feeling one, then another crack. He spun Kell around and ran him full-face into the side of the Cadillac, spun Kell around again and drove his knee up into Kell's crotch, then again and then jammed his right shoulder up tight under Kell's chin and pinned him against the car and went to work on Kell's middle with both fists. . . .

Chino finally got Stryker loose from Kell by kicking Stryker's feet from under him, then falling on Stryker, pinning him, shouting. "ENOUGH, COL, ENOUGH, ENOUGH, YOU'LL KILL HIM!"

16—CONVICTION

Stryker could not believe the speed with which everything happened after Chino pulled him off Kell.

That is, he could not believe it afterwards, when he had all the time in the world to think about it.

The events began ordinarily enough: Zenner radioed for assistance and an ambulance, which carried Kell to the hospital prison ward where he was booked on every charge Bellon could think of which might apply: illegal possession of explosives (the suitcases had been recovered at the airport), possession of illegal firearms and apparatus (the sawed-off shotgun and the silencer), interstate transportation of explosives and illegal firearms, burglary of auto by explosives, maiming and disfiguring (Colleen Stryker had not yet died), fraudulent use of stolen driver's license, registering under alias name with malicious intent, conspiracy to murder, and Murder I.

Chino also booked Sam and Jugs after they had been treated in hospital. Sam went in for conspiracy to commit bank robbery, bank robbery, maiming and disfiguring, conspiracy to murder, and Murder I, 2 counts (Patrolman Southwell and Doris Stryker). Jugs, the big-bosomed TV "Star", whose real name was Ethel Sale, was booked on various aiding, abetting, and accessory before and after the fact charges and conspiracy.

Stryker spent an hour with his mother-in-law at the hospital. Colleen's condition remained grave. During a four-hour operation a team of surgeons sewed her foot back on, but admitted the ankle would have no articulation: the running child would run no more.

When Stryker turned his attention to the arrangements for Doris, he felt sick and hollow with lead weight across the back of his neck. And his mother-in-law finally blew

—became hysterical and was herself hospitalized under heavy sedation.

Stryker saw the mortician and made the arrangements himself, then went back to his office. He had been there hardly fifteen minutes, just beginning his reports, when the phone rang. It was Don Pickett.

"Colin, get the hell out of there."

"What?"

"That fucking Peters filed a civil rights case against you and the assistant U.S. district attorney took it. Peters and Gordan are on the way over now to arrest you."

"You're joking, Don."

"Like hell. Get out of there, Stryker, find you a lawyer and see what kind of deal you can make." Pickett hung up.

Stryker grabbed his coat and took off for the Chief of Detectives' office. He never made it. In the hallway outside DC Seamon's office, he met Seamon and Peters and SA Ellis Gordan.

Peculiarly, five newsmen just happened to be there, armed with cameras, representing both major newspapers and all three TV stations in the city.

The moment Stryker came in sight, the TV cameramen flicked on their floods, and the newspaper photographers' strobes began flashing.

Peters actually drew his revolver. He made Stryker spread against the wall, like any crummy asshole, while Gordan searched, taking Stryker's Python, handcuffs, ammo pouch, and credentials, all of which he turned over to Seamon. Then he took out his own handcuffs and tied Stryker down.

Peters struck a fierce pose, stood on his tiptoes, and recited Stryker's rights according to the formula, all three TV microphones thrust into his face. Then he made a speech: carrying a badge made no man immune to laws of the land. Men who carried badges and violated laws they had sworn to uphold would suffer the same penalties as every other criminal! Wrong cops who violated their trust, the duty, honor, integrity of law enforcement, were the lowest of all scum . . . or words to that effect. . . .

145

The newsmen began a barrage of shrill questions, most relating to the fact that the persons whose rights Stryker had allegedly violated were those accused of murdering Mrs. Stryker and the sergeant's daughter as well as Patrolman Southwell.

Peters answered primly, "The law is very clear on that. There is *no*, I repeat, *no* justification for such brutally unprofessional conduct. A law enforcement officer must be above personal involvement, regardless what provocation he may have. The law is quite explicit on that."

In one of those abrupt silences that happen amidst pandemonium, a voice cut through the air like a knife, *"You bet, you fat little gutless wonder! Someone blew up your family, you'd be too fuckin yellow to go after them!"*

Peters' face flushed scarlet and his mouth worked and he finally shouted, "Get that man's name, get that man's name!"

Everyone in the hallway laughed, except Peters and Gordan and John The Baptist.

The newsmen hit Peters with more questions, this time related to the fact that Peters had stated The Bank of the Rockies case closed, yet Borchia and Sale had been booked on charges arising from that case. Peters retreated behind standard doctrine. "No comment."

"How can you have no comment," demanded Burr Cohen, a graying newsman with a cynical face and whiskey breath, "when Borchia and Sale are in jail on those charges?"

"Ah, if our investigation shows the case merits reopening, we shall do so."

"You mean it's a bum rap? Is that why Stryker's been arrested?"

"I have no further comment. Now, gentlemen, if you will excuse me——"

"You rotten little shit!" the same voice cut through again. *"Sleep well tonight!"*

Again everyone laughed, and Cohen jumped Peters again. "Is it true there is great personal animosity between you and Stryker? That you've been running a background check on him? That you've had him under surveillance and a tap on his home telephone?"

As the questions rumbled from the man, the others grew quieter, then absolutely silent. The only sounds in the hallway were grinding TV cameras and expectant breathing. "I'll repeat the questions, if you—"

Peters had gone blood red in the face again, then white, as though a huge needle had punctured his body and bled him dry. His jaw waggled and his lips trembled; he swallowed convulsively. He clenched his jaws and finally managed to speak: "Those are the most baseless, slanderous accusations—"

"Just one goddam minute!" Cohen snapped. "I asked questions. I made no accusations."

Peters turned on Seamon savagely. "What kind of place do you run here? Goddamit, get this hallway cleared!"

"Fuck you!" shouted the same unknown cutting voice. *"This ain't the Fuck-Buddy-Institute!"*

Hardly anyone laughed this time; everyone stared at Peters, waiting for him to have a heart attack. He glared at Seamon again, then nodded to Gordan and they began shoving Stryker along the hallway with his hands cuffed behind him.

The cameras recorded every detail.

They interrogated Stryker for an hour, during which Stryker said nothing. Then they took Stryker before the Federal Magistrate, who found reasonable cause to believe the stated violations had occurred and that Stryker had committed those violations. At the request of the assistant U.S. attorney, Stryker's bond was set at $25,000, in lieu of which he was committed to jail. Two U.S. Marshals took custody of Stryker, removed Gordan's handcuffs, and put their own on, then marched Stryker to the county jail and booked him.

Stryker did not know how many times he'd been through the procedure from the other side: empty pockets, count money, inventory every item on the big tan envelope, take his belt and shoestrings so he couldn't commit suicide by

147

hanging himself; he was fingerprinted, photographed, interviewed for personal data—name, age, date of birth, place of birth, height, weight, color of eyes and hair, marks, scars, tattoos, home address, place of employment. . . .

He was taken down the hall, given a haircut, made to shower with strong lye-base soap after a dousing with spray to kill any lice, crabs, fleas, or other body parasites. During the whole time, Stryker did not speak except to answer the identification-and-records officer's questions, and say "Thanks," to those jailers, turnkeys, and the jail warden who told him how sorry they were, having to treat him this way. They all shook his hand.

After his shower, Stryker got a pair of jail coveralls much too small for him, then was taken up to the top floor of the jail and put into solitary confinement . . . for his own protection. Had he been thrown into the regular jail population, he might have lived as long as two, possibly three hours, because of his size and strength. Certainly by the end of the fourth hour the assholes would have worn him down and stomped him to death.

Ten minutes after Stryker was put into his cell, Gordan and Peters arrived and attempted another interrogation. Stryker spoke only twice.

He told Peters: "That was a beautiful speech you made. I wonder why you don't apply it to yourself. You *know* if you tell yourself the truth, the only reason I'm in here is because you have a personal hardon for me."

To Gordan he said, "Aren't you the agent who got a disciplinary transfer for trying to kidnap a Mexican national across the border to make a case against another cop?"

While Peters and Gordan were in the cell, Seamon personally served departmental charges on Stryker. He was suspended indefinitely without pay pending the outcome of criminal charges now lodged against him. With a smile, Seamon said, "Of course that also means immediate cancellation of your group insurance. It's too bad about your daughter." He smiled again and shouted for the turnkey to let him out. The FBI also left, seeing the hopelessness of getting a statement from Stryker.

An hour later the assistant U.S. attorney arrived with a deal. If Stryker would implicate Bellon in a violation of civil rights, Stryker would get an immediate reduction of his bond. Stryker did not bother to reply. The DA stayed an hour and Stryker never spoke a word. He only heard the man's voice as a background noise, like a radio that's always on. Stryker's thoughts remained fixed on two things: getting out of jail and paying Colleen's medical/doctor bills.

At the moment, he had no hope whatever of getting out of jail. He did not have, and had no way of getting one-tenth of his bond, $2500, which a professional bondsman would require, in cash, to bail him out.

So long as he remained in the slammer, the second question remained totally academic.

The DA finally got Stryker's attention: "I'll arrange for you to attend your wife's funeral."

"Fuck you."

"What?"

"If you think I'm going to my wife's funeral in handcuffs, with a marshal on each side of me, you're an even stupider shitheel than you've already proved yourself. A cheap chickenshit *dupe*. Does Peters hold your hand while you pee?"

"Listen, Stryker, I don't—"

"Get the hell out of here, you smallbore puke," Stryker shouted, and when the guard came Stryker gestured toward the DA as though indicating garbage in his cell. "Get him out of here and don't let him in again."

After the DA left, a hack named Grady came to the cell with a heavy paper bag full of magazines, a deck of cards, some paperback books, five foil pouches of chewing tobacco, a dozen excellent cigars, matches, a transistor radio, a pair of coveralls that fit—and the latest word from the hospital: Colleen Stryker had regained consciousness briefly, and her condition was somewhat improved, but she seemed to be blind. "I thought you'd druther hear it from me, sarge, than over the radio."

"Thanks, Grady, really."

149

"Chino'n some-a the fellers sent the stuff. Anything you want?"

"I could use twenty-five hundred bucks," Stryker said, making himself smile.

"I think they're workin' on that, too, sarge."

Stryker shook his head. "No, tell'm not do that, will you, Grady?"

"Chino wants to see you."

"Will they let him in?"

"Not supposed to. That DA said no visitors, period. Lessn'n you get a lawyer."

Stryker shrugged. "I guess that rips it."

"Well, no. . . ." Grady grinned. "The Warden says he thinks that fruiter around on the other side we gotta keep up here so he don't get raped, well, Jack thinks he's probably a fugitive and Chino better have a talk with him, Chino bein' in Fugitive Squad'n all." He grinned again.

"I bet he *is* an FFJ, sure's hell," Stryker said.

Chino spent twenty minutes with the fruiter, and damned if he didn't drop his mud and admit being wanted for hot checks in Idaho. Then Chino came around to Stryker's cell. "We're getting Santiago Ximenez to represent you. I don't have to tell you he's the best." Chino grinned. "He's boxed our ears plenty over the years when we thought we had a lock on cases. Remember?"

Stryker nodded. Ximenez was the best lawyer in the state so far as most cops and DAs were concerned. He'd lost few cases and never a capital case when the prosecutor had gone for the death penalty . . . back in those days.

After a moment, Stryker said, "No, I don't want you to do that, Chino."

"*What!* God'l Mighty, Colin!"

"Look, get your head on like mine. I've got no money. We carried no insurance on Doris or the baby, except group hospital, only on me in case I got blown up, being a cop. Her father is dead and her mother's got a little monthly income off his retirement, social security and some insurance. My Mom's got a little dough, probably, and she would sell every head of stock and mortage that old

150

starve-out ranch if I'd let her. But all that would do is throw her into a bind she could never pay out if she lived another seventy-eight years. I won't let her do that. So I sure as hell can't let *you* guys do what I won't let my own people do."

"I've got a little money," Chino said defensively.

"Damned little. A single guy like you gets raped on income taxes, and I know you whip-out for your mother every check. None of the other guys are in any better shape. . . . Tell me the truth. . . . What's Santiago want for a retainer?"

Chino squirmed and looked at the floor. "Well . . . quite a bit."

"Two grand cash."

"Almost. Eighteen hundred."

"And when that's paid, it's gone, buddy; just like it's gone, forever, if he did happen to get my bond reduced and then you guys came up with enough dough for a bailbondsman. Maybe I could pay you back part of it by selling out everything I own. House, what furniture the explosion didn't destroy. I could probably get ten bucks for what's left of my car from a junk dealer. More likely have to pay someone to haul it off." Stryker touched Chino's arm. "Don't think I don't appreciate it. You know I do. . . . But you see what I mean?"

"Yeah, I guess so." Chino looked around the bare cell, bars and concrete deck, seatless toilet, iron bunk hanging by chains from the steel wall, with a thin mattress and one threadbare blanket. "God, I just can't stand thinking of you *here*."

"We've been worse places, Chino . . . out in Nam."

Chino nodded dully. Then he looked up. "I almost forgot. I'm moving into your pad, OK?"

"Why?"

"Soon as you got busted, they pulled the guard off. When I heard, I drove out there and found one of your lousy neighbors carrying off a TV set." Chino's laugh expressed absolute cynicism. "Said he was just taking care of

151

it for you. Funny thing. He had already taken a file to the goddam serial number."

"I guess you'd better move in if that's how it's going. And thanks again."

"Anything else I can do?"

"I hate to ask, but—"

"Frig that, Colin. Anything, dammit!"

"Could you go see my Mom? You know where the ranch is, way to hell'n gone out in Valencia County, no phone, and she goes a week, ten days sometimes without turning on the radio if the damned lightplant's working at all. She never goes to town for the mail and newspapers more than once a week. There's a good chance she doesn't know about this yet, and I'd like her to hear it from you, the whole story. If she's heard it, I want you to explain what she *must* do. Keep the livestock and the ranch, no selling, no mortgages, nothing. OK?"

"I'll go tonight."

"Who's running the Squad?"

"I wish you hadn't asked. . . . Southerlund. Seamon's orders."

"Christ."

"I don't believe He's paying attention today."

The case of U.S. vs. Colin MacGregor Stryker proceeded with all due haste. His court-appointed attorney was a small, rotund, kinky-haired, bespectacled young man named Maurice Gavin. Until his assignment to the Stryker case, Gavin's total experience in criminal law consisted of losing five cases in city traffic court and losing two cases in county court, one involving first offense DWI, the other a wife-beating.

After their first meeting Stryker told Gavin he need not bother returning for more conferences; he'd see him in court. Much relieved, Gavin gathered his papers and unmarked notepad and stuffed them into his expensive green leather attaché case while he shouted for the turnkey. At the door, he stopped and faced Stryker, frowning. "Uh, how do you want me to plead you?"

"Not guilty."

"Do you think that's wise?"

"Hasn't anyone ever told you about pleading?"

Gavin peered through his glasses, blinking.

"Never admit anything, lawyer. If your wife catches you on top of another woman, swear you didn't have it in."

"Wha—? . . . *Oh!* Oh, yes, hah-hah, quite amusing. I must remember that one."

"I think they've probably heard it before, lawyer."

Seven weeks later, Stryker went on trial.

During the intervening weeks, Colleen survived. At first the doctors had hoped the blindness to be temporary, resulting from pressures on the brain caused by the various skull fractures. But as one remedial procedure or operation followed another and the blindness remained, they finally concluded the blindness permanent. A specialist agreed, summoned and paid by Bellon and Stryker's mother.

Upon learning this news, Doris' mother suffered a stroke and became a bedridden invalid.

Colleen's hospital/doctor bills now amounted to more than $12,000, and the hospital administrator began sending Stryker daily demands for partial payment, accompanied by insinuated threats to turn Colleen Stryker, age four, over to county welfare authorities. Bellon learned of this from Jail Warden Jack Canady who inspected, as was his duty, all Stryker's mail. Bellon made a call upon the hospital administrator, and the administrator puffed out his chest and wiped his glasses and strode around his wall-to-wall carpeted office and explained the facts of life to Bellon.

About mid-afternoon the following day, the administrator's wife called her husband, almost hysterical. Since shortly after 8 a.m., she had been visited and given citations by the sanitation department, the city housing inspection office, the fire department, and given four traffic tickets by various cops while on a shopping trip to Winrock Center. The administrator told his wife to settle down, called his mother-in-law and asked her to go over. He then called the Mayor and made an appointment. He went out and drove toward downtown. In the first two miles he got three tickets for various violations of traffic laws. When stopped the fourth time, less than a block from city hall, he refused to sign the ticket and warned the cop, "I'm on my way to see the mayor!"

The cop said, "When you see the fucker, tell him we need a raise." Then he called for a tow and placed the administrator under arrest. At that moment, Chino Bellon pulled to a halt behind the motorcycle, got out, and came forward. "What say, Polack?"

"Hi, Chino."

"Well, hello, Mr. Administrator! What's this?"

"I think you know very well."

"Oh?"

"My wife and I are being harassed unmercifully and I—"

"You mean like Colleen Stryker's father is being har-

154

assed, particularly by demands for payment and threats to put his daughter in a welfare home?"

"I see. . . ."

"Do you?"

"I think so."

"You'd better be sure."

"I have an appointment with the mayor."

"Let me tell you something about the mayor. He's a real screwy guy. For a politician, he's plumb damned *weird*. Once when I was on motors, I stopped him for speeding, not knowing, you see, it was him. You know what happened? He told me if I *didn't* give him a ticket, he'd have my ass before God got the news. And you know what else? He *paid* that sumbitchin ticket!"

"All right."

"You're sure, are you?"

"Absolutely."

"OK, you give me those tickets you got, and I'll be around to see you in your office tomorrow. You give me any other citations you or members of your family might have gotten, *along with a letter* to Colin Stryker that he should not worry about his daughter. I'll take care of your small problems when you take care of Stryker's big one. Deal?"

"You know this is blackmail, pure and simple. I could have you in the same cell with Stryker."

"I know this, you lousy son of a bitch—you resemble a man about as much as I do a fuckin polar bear. I tried reasoning with you yesterday, and you came on with some horseshit! A hospital's not a charitable institution. Which makes you a liar. You've got twenty-nine charity patients in your place now! You write them off taxwise and get a ton of publicity and public relations running their pictures in the papers and on TV and in trade journals. . . . And, bigshot, if you *really* want leaned on, I'll personally see to it your wife knows about that beautiful black receptionist with the unbelievable ass and a certain motel in Moriarty."

Chino turned to Stogowski. "Polack, put the iron on him and I'll haul his ass to the slammer."

"NO! WAIT!"

"On what?"

"If you'll come back to the hospital with me, I'll give you the letter now."

The trial took just one day. The DA built a routine case. Among those who testified for the prosecution were Deputy Chief Seamon, Det/1 Southerlund, Salvatore Borrzi, alias Big Sam Borchia; Ethel Sale, SAIC Peters, and SA Gordan, FBI; Det/2 Zenner (reluctantly), and several home-owners and motorists who witnessed some part or all of Stryker's attack upon Kell. The prosecution offered in evidence a deposition taken from Kell, who was still in hospital and unable to appear in person.

Defense Attorney Gavin's ineptitude became so embarrassing that Stryker finally stopped him from attempting to cross-examine. Stryker did not take the stand. The jury went out and came back twenty minutes later with guilty verdicts on all three counts, violating the civil rights of Kell, Sale, and Borchia. The judge polled the jurors individually. He set Stryker's sentencing for two weeks later, after the Federal Probation Officer had completed his investigation and made his report and recommendations.

Stryker got two years on each count, with six months' hard-time and the remainder on probation, concurrent sentences. That same afternoon U.S. Marshals delivered him by auto to the Federal Correctional Institution at La Tuna, four miles south of the New Mexico-Texas state line at Anthony.

Following his brief term in isolation, required of all prisoners upon arrival, Stryker was turned into the general prison population. Here he was no longer personally known and universally respected by every guard, turnkey, jailor, and the warden. In fact, the opposite: he was a wrong cop. The prison officials made sure the word got around. The prison population was almost 75% Mexican nationals or Mexican-American, some blacks, a few Indians, the rest Anglos. The proportions among the officials were almost exactly the same, with Anglos occupying most of the upper echelon jobs.

Stryker was put to work in the fields, chopping and irrigating cotton, lettuce, tomatoes, and other produce. The FCI sat on the side of a long slope between I–10 and Highway 80 along the Rio Grande. He could see west to Tres Hermanas, The Three Sisters Mountains, at Columbus, New Mexico and the Floridas at Deming on smogfree days, with the Portrillos in the foreground. To the east rose the Franklins, divided from the Organ Mountains by Anthony Gap. Southwest lay Mexico, El Paso-Juárez to the south.

It was October now. He had been given credit for his time in jail awaiting trial. If he lost no good time, he would be turned out sometime in January. If he volunteered for certain programs, gave blood, etc., he would earn additional "good time," so it was possible, barely, he could turn out just before Christmas.

Stryker did not count on it.

His second day in the general population after isolation provided him with an indication of how things would go.

He was a wrong cop.

Every con in the joint who remembered the cops who'd busted them centered their frustration and anger upon Stryker. In fact, there were four cons whom Stryker had been personally responsible for sending to this prison. They agitated. One worked as a trustie in the chowline and poured scalding coffee on Stryker's hand. He dropped his cup and the hack cursed him with filthy obscenities in Spanish, and everyone laughed and made equally crude remarks, knowing Stryker's Spanish was as fluent as or better than their own.

Stryker only looked at the man, memorizing his face, and saw the uncertainty that suddenly clouded the trustie's eyes.

At the table where he was assigned to eat all his meals, two blacks, one almost as large as Stryker himself, ruled with undisputed authority. On those days when certain foods the blacks liked were served, other cons at the table

157

automatically passed their portions to Pink Davis and Treasure Blades Monroe. Pink was so called because the backs of his inky hands had irregular pink spots on them, a birthmark. Blades is slang for teeth in certain societies, and Monroe had several gold caps and fillings; thus, Treasure Blades.

That night dessert was canned peaches, and as soon as each man sat down he passed his tray to the head of the table where Davis or Monroe spooned off the peaches and syrup. When Stryker sat down, the man at his right murmured, "Pass your tray up."

"Huh?"

"Your tray. Pass it up."

Stryker began eating. Across the table Indian Joe spoke in Navajo, of which Stryker had learned the fundamentals as a boy working on the ranch with Mexican and Indian cowboys. Joe said, "You're supposed to pass your tray so the blacks can take you peaches."

"You have not passed yours."

"No."

"Then?"

"I am exempt."

"How so?"

Joe shrugged. He began eating. Stryker asked again. Joe did not answer. Then Stryker remembered Joe was doing life for double murder on a reservation, having killed his adulterous wife and her lover. For a Navajo in prison, the man who killed him would do him the greatest possible favor, Stryker knew. Too often had he seen Navajos leave the reservation, learn good trades as welders, plumbers, naval officers, computer programmers . . . and then go back to the blanket, live in a filthy stinking *hogan,* one pair of Levi's and a single shirt their only possessions. They would work at odd jobs, on or off the reservation, get whiskey money, get falling-down, knee-walking drunk, serve out their time if they got arrested, and go back to the blanket again. If asked why they had thrown it all away, they would reply with some obscure muttering about not wishing to be possessed, to be owned, which most Anglos could not understand, but Stryker did. His job had owned him. It had, finally, killed his wife and blinded his baby and put him in prison. He had seen other cops divorced, become alcoholics, a few drug addicts, many suicides. What white men called success an Indian could very well call selling out.

The table became quiet as Stryker continued eating. "Hey, you, honkey pig motherf—!" Pink said. "Get them motherf— peaches down here, man."

Stryker ignored him and kept eating.

"Hey, man, you heah me?"

Stryker kept eating.

"You sumbitch motherf—!" said Treasure Blades, the huge one, a dominant force in the whole prison population. Except for a few "made" mob guys who remained in continuous isolation because they were snitches, Monroe enjoyed the most privileged status in the institution. A simple matter of peace in the family. The hacks found it easier to let Monroe have his way to an extraordinary degree than to face constant racial conflicts within the prison and unremitting racism accusations from outside. Treasure Blades and Pink kept things "cool" so long as they were kept happy, and the officials found it worth the effort.

It would have been better for everyone had the officials explained this to Stryker rather than requiring him to discover it on his own.

Stryker did not raise his head and kept on with eating motions as he spoke. "Don't try running over the top of me. You can't. Leave me alone and I'll leave you alone."

"Whoo-ee, listen-a *that* sheeit!" Pink said, laughing. "An wha-chew gonna do, Cap'n suh, we *don* leave you lone?" He howled with glee. "You gonna *rest* us? Gonna throw us no-count nigger spades in *jail!*"

Now everyone at the table laughed.

A hack came by, commanding, "All right, knock off the shit, you got three minutes to finish!"

Stryker finished his meat, fried beans, potatoes, and half his coffee and began eating his peaches.

Indian Joe looked up and shook his head sadly, but

159

Stryker saw the warmth in the black eyes and the bare hint of smile twisting one corner of Joe's mouth.

They finished eating and went on the yard.

Stryker saw them shaping up, Pink and Monroe and their followers. He knew it had to happen and he felt glad, unafraid. Sooner done, sooner settled.

They moved toward him, and "crowded" him. An emaciated addict had been assigned the job, but with wild-eyed eagerness he came on too fast, too strong, reckless. Stryker chopped him across the throat, grabbed the bony wrist of the hand holding the stolen spoon ground and shaped to a razor-edged point. Stryker snapped the thin wrist like a dry stick and got the weapon. He dropped the screeching dupe and shot his body through the crowd. Before the stunned Treasure Blades Monroe knew what happened, he no longer had a left eye. Stryker looped his right arm around Monroe's neck in a hammerlock, jerked his head, stabbed the pointed, razorlike spoon into Monroe's eye.

In the same instant, Stryker released Monroe and drove his elbow directly into Pink's solar plexus, dropping him unconscious on his back. Stryker put the weapon in Pink's palm, then stood on the fat wrist and watched the hacks come running.

No one except Stryker ever knew what really happened. It went down too fast. No one believed Pink had put out Monroe's eye. Everyone knew Flaco *had* the shiv but got a ruptured larnyx and broken arm. No one knew for *sure* Stryker had done any of this . . . when questioned . . . because they were afraid. Fear ruled on the yard. A new and more powerful Stud was on the yard now. Stryker. No one dared speak against him.

He was never bothered again.

Stryker did his time hard, one day at a time, working in the fields, sweating, skin blackening under the desert sun though fall ended and winter came on. He took no favors, accepted no privileges, cooperated without comment, submitted to tests and evaluations and gave blood. He never spoke except when it was required. He did the hard common labor in the fields, trimmed off twenty pounds, hands blistering, blisters breaking, gummy with blood, more blisters, calluses, calluses on top of calluses.

Bellon met him outside the front gate on Christmas Eve and hardly recognized him, all sunburned muscle and bone and jungle instinct hardened and honed by imprisonment. They drove to the ranch. Stryker's mother had Colleen, having simply picked her up and walked out with her one day when visiting, watching the hospital staff deliberately neglect the child.

Stryker now felt beyond all emotion but discovered himself wrong when he picked his daughter up and she looked at him with sightless eyes. She smiled and said, "How was prison, Dad? Pretty bad, huh?"

"Not so bad as being blind," Stryker sobbed, glad that his mother, Colleen MacGregor Stryker, had concealed nothing from his child.

"It's nae so bad, Dad, since Gramaw taught me the hoose, so I nae fall over things now." Her accent was broad; she spoke Gaelic to her Gramaw.

Chino had to turn away and walk outside, and he did not return for an hour; he could not stand it. He lit a coal oil lamp in the bunkhouse and smoked a cigarette and took a belt from the bottle of Old Parr. He drank and smoked as he read over the thick sheaf of typewritten notes he'd prepared for Colin.

Chino knew what he had done, was doing, would continue doing, if necessary, was wrong. He owed his allegiance to the department, not to a man once his boss and now an ex-convict still on probation.

But Chino had not been able to settle for that. Where his real allegiance lay, what his duty demanded of him, was contained in the oath of office he took when he graduated from Academy: ". . . preserve the peace and tranquility, protect the lives and property of the people of this city, this state, and this nation, against all enemies whomsoever. . . ."

Stryker had taken the same oath. Yet Stryker had gone

to prison while Borchia, and Ethel Sale, and the bomber Kell all went free. They had never even gone to trial.

That neither Kell nor Sam and his mistress would ever go to trial did not mean they had escaped punishment. Bellon did not know what Stryker intended to do; he had never asked him. He dared not. He could only extend his help so far, accomplish what he could.

That had not been inconsiderable.

Using leads furnished by Stryker when Bellon visited him at La Tuna every other Sunday, Bellon exposed John The Baptist Seamon's womanizing. Seamon's wife left him and shortly thereafter he retired. A month later he suicided.

Bellon personally took care of Southerlund, setting him up after Seamon retired and could no longer protect him, and got Southerlund fired for dereliction of duty, multiple offenses. Zenner was left alone; he'd been a reluctant and hostile witness. The DA had to prize answers from Zenn on the stand, but he'd had no choice but tell the truth and Stryker did not hold that against him.

The media had taken care of Peters and Gordan. The elderly, cynical reporter named Cohen kept after Peters about his harassment of Stryker, and while Stryker soaked in jail other newsmen took it up, finally forcing an investigation. The investigation was conducted by an Inspector from Bureau HQ, a man even more ruthless than Peters himself. Faced with the choice of demotion and transfer or retirement, Peters retired and moved to California. Ellis Gordan simply vanished. When asked about Gordan's fate —transfer, resignation, dismissal, the new SAIC kept repeating, "No comment."

The assistant U.S. attorney learned to his dismay the real price of Stryker's conviction after he'd let the FBI hustle him into mashing Stryker.

How distinctly *did* he remember, in frequent moments of recall, the old federal judge's query when he first went in with the case: "Are you quite sure you want to do this?"

"Positively!"

Then, when he began preparing his cases against Borchia, Sale, and Kell, the judge said, "I'm sorry, but I won't hear the cases; no federal judge will."

Dumbfounded, the assistant U.S. DA said, "But *why?*"

"Because you had to have Stryker. You got him. Don't you recall? He's in the penitentiary now. Your entire case was built upon Stryker's violation of these people's civil rights. His conviction *tainted* every facet of the evidence, made all evidence suspect, illegal search and seizure, duress, coercion, etc. Poisoned the vine, so all fruit therefrom is tainted."

"But, my *God!* judge, this Kell beast murdered a woman and blinded a child. There is no question now that Borchia authored the bank robbery and is therefore guilty of murdering Officer Southwell."

"Quite true. But you and Mr. Peters wanted Stryker. Do you recall what I asked you when you brought the case to me?"

"Yessir."

"I'm glad that you do. I think it only fair to tell you in person that I have recommended your dismissal. . . . And now, good day, young man. . . ."

That took care of the smallbore creeps, and Stryker saved the others for himself. They owed him personally and he intended to see they honored their debts.

That evening, after putting his daughter to bed, Stryker discovered his circumstances were far better than he'd supposed.

He had money.

Unknown to him, his mother-in-law carried an insurance policy on Doris, which she collected when Kell murdered Stryker's wife.

The old woman died after another stroke while Stryker chopped prison cotton, leaving everything to Stryker and her grandchild.

Stryker ignored his mother's accent as she told him: "I have a man looking after your affairs, and Chino looks after *him*. Your mother-in-law left a tidy sum, almost thirty thousand dollars, with Doris' insurance to the back of that, fifteen thousand. Her hoose was paid out, and I have it rented now to people who want to buy. Through Chino, I paid all your bills with ranch money and we will settle up when it is convenient with you. Chino had your hoose repaired, the wall rebuilt, and it is rented also to people who wish to buy. From the both you should realize no less than twenty thousand dollars if you bide. On quick-sale, no more than half that, I think."

Stryker faced Bellon. "Do you want my house?"

"Huh?"

"You can have it if you want it. I'll sign it over. You take up the payments."

"Where would you live?"

"I couldn't live there."

"Sure. . . . Naw, I don't think so, Colin; but thanks."

"You may get married some day. Be a good start."

Bellon looked into his glass of Old Parr and cold wellwater. He shook his head. "I couldn't live there either. I moved soon's I got the wall fixed."

"I've got to repay you somehow."

Bellon looked up. For an instant, Stryker saw a flash of undiluted anger in the deep brown eyes; then Bellon shook his head, and took a sip of whiskey. Stryker never again mentioned owing Bellon.

"Now what are you about, son?" asked Colleen MacGregor Stryker.

Stryker looked at Bellon, and Bellon got up and went back to the bunkhouse.

"You know what I must do, Momma."

"Aye, ye nae be a MacGregor, did ye nae." She poured a quarter inch of Scotch in her jelly glass and drank it neat. "Weel ye nae go in preeson agin?"

"No way, ever."

His mother nodded. "A good thing your Dad's passed on these many years, for he would hae doon it h'self."

"I was afraid *you* would."

"Aye, and so I would except they put you insie the short time. When weel ye gae?"

"Not for a while. I don't want them to know I'm coming."

"Aye!"

"Treacherous as a Campbell, Momma—when I must."

She nodded again. Then she told him about the money, when he was ready to use it. Stryker went to the door and shouted for Chino. He came in and they sat down, poured, raised their glasses, "Merry Christmas!" They touched glasses and drank.

Bellon stayed over the next day while Colleen opened her gifts and learned to manage the tricycle despite her stiff left ankle and blindness. They had a big turkey dinner, a wild one weighing forty-six pounds that Paul Stalking Deer, one of the cowpunchers, had shot two days earlier. They ate in the cowboys' cookshack, a tradition going back to 1927, the year Colleen MacGregor got off the morning train in Magdalena, New Mexico; a big, strapping, buxom, inky-haired, green-eyed Scotswoman from so far back in the Highlands she spoke almost no English, a contract bride. After a bath and change she married Ian Stryker; they climbed upon the seat of a wagon loaded with supplies, and she did not see town again for almost three years, while carrying Duncan, after the births of Malcolm and Rob. She was too busy having babies, cooking for her family and crew, learning English, Spanish, Navajo and Apache, tending a one-acre vegetable garden, carrying fifty gallons of water three hundred yards from the windmill to the house every day, for cooking, washing, drinking, laundry; making soap from lye and ashes, re-soling boots, making shirts, bedding, underclothing; jerking beef and venison, canning fruits from the orchard and vegetables from her garden. During her spare time she learned to read and write English as well as speak it passably. Stryker could never figure out why his mother spoke almost flawless Spanish, without accent, excellent Navajo, adequate Apache, but still burrr-ed hell out of her English, except that as a Scot she had had little use for "those people who lived to the south." When her husband died, she stuck him in the ground and took over running the ranch; she'd been doing the books and managing the affairs since the crash in '29, and, mainly due to her efforts, they did not lose the place during the Depression years. Of her seven sons, three survived: Colin, Brice, Duncan. Brice was mostly worthless, a hustler, a con man, who traded land and cattle and airplanes and other properties along the border, undoubtedly did some smuggling both ways. After a highly successful college and fifteen-year NFL career as a linebacker, Duncan now coached in the pro league, one of the coast teams.

Rob, the eldest, had managed to get himself shot from ambush by a jealous husband in Quemado. Walt got tangled in a terrible wreck when he roped a two-year-old steer off a green bronc and the horse went crazy and bucked into a barbed wire fence, fell with Walt under him, kicking, biting, lunging, and a strand of barbed wire sawed through Walt's windpipe. Malcolm, a Navy carrier pilot, died of torture and starvation in a North Korean POW camp; and

Greg, the youngest, suffered an almost identical fate at the hands of the North Vietnamese.

After the big Christmas dinner, the cowpunchers went to town: Paul Stalking Deer, Juán Lozano, and Billy Mac-Lelan threw their warbags in the back of Juán's old pickup and lit out for the bright lights with huge thirsts, necks bulging with backed-up semen, money in their jeans, eager to run and play with dedicated ferocity till they went broke, got thrown in jail, or otherwise ended their party in town. Mrs. Stryker told them to be back the third of January, by which she meant the fifth, if possible. She also swore she would *not!* come to town and bail them out or advance any wages, but they knew she would if they got in a bind.

Chino also left shortly after the Christmas dinner. He turned over the thick sheaf of papers to Stryker with a sense of guilt, yet with a feeling of serving justice. Stryker studied the report after putting his daughter to bed. . . .

Sam had played his notoriety to advantage, having hired himself a PR man, doing the Colombo bit: forming a sort of Italian-American anti-defamation society. He did not go so far as picketing police headquarters, but he did buy additional local TV time and pay some household names extremely high fees for one-minute spot announcements praising the society on station breaks and during the late movies. Business at Bella Napoli went upwards steadily, with a mostly new staff. All those who'd given statements about Sam dining with the bank robbers lost their jobs, and two of them had vanished, Huero Garcia the waiter and the busboy who'd cleaned up the table.

Ethel Sale continued her daily TV show. She got off many cracks about police brutality and loaded her guest list with dissident militants of every hue, persuasion, goal, objective, and belief—so long as the central theme remained "police state tactics." Her ratings fell out the bottom and Sam Borchia's construction company came to a standstill, so he told her to knock it off, he wasn't running a local edition of the Cavett Forum.

Sam's wife departed, taking at least $250,000 cash, all

167

her jewelry, furs, expensive clothing, and the Mark IV which had replaced the Merc that Chino Bellon devastated. Sam moved Ethel into the house.

But what Stryker found most curious of all. . .

Kell had stayed on in the city after finally being discharged from hospital. He'd also moved in with Sam, and Sam paid all the bills.

Bellon wrote in his report to Stryker:

"Kell evidently found a bird's nest on the ground with Sam. The three of them are so inextricably bound together none dares offend either of the others for fear of death or imprisonment. The immunity law gives each power over the other two, so they are stuck with one another and stick with one another, none trusting the others, using one another, milking one another, and by now I am sure hating each other. . . ."

These circumstances made a routine—three people who mistrust one another so much, yet all have work and diversions and must establish a pattern, a routine, a schedule, or nothing got done. Stryker memorized the salient facts, then put Chino's report into the flaming fireplace, one page at a time. He knew exactly what he was going to do and exactly how he would do it and when, after a few arrangements.

A month after his release, Stryker reported to his parole officer in Albuquerque, then returned directly to the ranch and resumed his work, cowboying: seeing after the stock, putting out cottonseed cake and hay for feed, blocks of salt, chopping ice in the tanks with an axe so the cattle could water, keeping the windmills running, repairing fence, pulling bogged cattle when a thaw came. It was not a particularly bad winter; they only suffered a 12-15% loss as best Mrs. Stryker could estimate before roundup. Every month on the appointed day, Stryker washed and shaved and put on clean jeans and shirt and jacket and his town hat and boots and drove to Albuquerque and reported to the parole officer. He drove directly home after lunch, with possibly a stop in Socorro or Magdalena to buy supplies, and just before going north from Highway 60 he stopped at the post office and got the mail and papers. He

168

did not drink, spoke to no one except his parole officer and those with whom he did business. Except for that monthly trip, Stryker did not leave the ranch. He saw the winter out, lips chapped and scaly, hands sore and numb, feet like blocks of ice, face seared raw by razor winds. He wrote no letters, received none.

In September, nine months since his release from La Tuna, Stryker made his first moves.

After reporting, he did not return directly home but went instead for a physical checkup. The doctor happened to be among those authorized by the FAA to issue pilot medical certificates and student pilot permits. Stryker had them in his pocket when he left. That afternoon, at a small inconspicuous airport some distance south down the river valley from Albuquerque, Stryker arranged for the purchase of a well-equipped 1959 Cessna 180 with a new airworthiness certificate. The trade included lessons, and he registered the Cessna in the ranch's name. He went home, discussed certain matters with his mother, and returned to the airport next day while she drove to the city. They met that night in the motel room he'd taken near the airport, and she handed over a cashier's check and $700 cash for his personal expenses. The next day he bought the airplane, began flying three hours a day, studying ground school at night. He took the written exam three weeks later and passed with a score of 92. Meantime he'd soloed, taken his dual cross-country, done his airwork and solo cross-countries, and two days after his report to the parole officer in October, Stryker took and passed his oral and flight exams and got his private pilot license. He flew the 180 miles to the ranch and landed on a dirt strip Juán and Billy had dragged clean of all brush and cactus with chained crossties behind a tractor. Stryker tied the airplane down, locked the controls, covered it with three large tarps, and went back to work cowboying.

Upon Stryker's release from FCI, La Tuna, Sam conferred with Kell and Ethel. As a result, he increased house

169

and ground guards from two men sundown to dawn to three men around the clock. Kell got a verified tough customer from Chi as their personal bodyguard/chauffeur.

But the months wore on.

Sam put the bent vice squad cop on the ear and he reported back, "The guy's a whipped hound. He's working like a friggin slave for his old lady on that worthless ranch over in Valencia County."

"I can't believe it," Kell said, fingertips touching the lumps on his jaw where the fractures healed irregularly despite the doctors' best efforts. "It's an act. He's playing it double-cool, waiting us out."

"Keep on it," Sam told the made cop.

Kenedy kept on it and found nothing. He knew Stryker's reporting day and picked him up on the outskirts of town and tailed him in, watched him park, followed him afoot into the federal building, saw him into the parole officer's, watched him emerge, a man the shadow of his former self, twenty or thirty pounds skinnier, eyes sunken, mouth like a scar, face chapped, hands rough and scaly, dressed in clean but worn old ranch clothing, driving a rattletrap pickup; and he followed Stryker out of town, the first two times all the way back to the ranch turnoff from Highway 60. After this repeated itself three and four and finally six months, the bent cop stopped bothering. When he reported to Sam, he said whatever he felt like saying; it did not matter because it was always the same. He was totally unaware that Stryker had noticed his surveillance within a mile after Kenedy tied onto him the first time, in January. And Stryker was equally aware when the surveillance ceased. He had not been a cop virtually all his adult life without learning elementary tactics for personal and professional survival, just as he had not survived combat in Korea and several tours in Nam through sheer luck or because God was on his side. . . .

Sam Borchia found himself in a bitchen money pinch, caused by his wife's departure with a quarter of a million dollars and all her valuables, the total inactivity of his construction company, supporting Kell and Ethel, his PR and advertising expenses, and Fess Waxmann's absconding with at least a hundred grand, leaving the loansharking operation in shambles—and a *ton* of cash his lawyers cost!

Sam found it increasingly unrealistic to keep a twenty-four-hour guard on the payroll, especially when Kenedy told him repeatedly that Stryker had lost his balls, would cause no trouble. Deep down, Sam did not believe this. He'd heard through his sources what happened at La Tuna. . . . Stryker could have been running the goddam joint, the most feared man inside, but Sam *wanted* to believe Stryker had caved in, and the tighter strapped he got for ready cash, the more he wanted to believe, the easier it became.

So he dismissed all guards but the guy Kell brought out from Chi, sending them to colleagues who could use and afford them.

Of course, Sam became careless; they all did, unable to keep continuously primed and ready for an attack when they saw no evidence whatever of any threat against themselves. And Kenedy kept downgrading Stryker with detailed descriptions of the man, a mere ghost of the absolute badass cop he'd once been.

No sweat, no problems, all A-OK! Hell, even Bellon had given up on it. Stryker was reduced to the point where his *mother* conducted his affairs for him, for Chrissake! Stryker had signed over a power of attorney to her. She sold his house, sold his mother-in-law's place. . . . Hell, Sam, forget him.

With all the other pressures, especially pinched for dough, suffering that goddam Kell twenty-four hours a day —he *knew* Ethel and Kell were making it behind his back, lousy bastards!

—Christ, just too much to keep track of . . . he had to get the shylocking back on a paying basis, but he had less than fifty grand on the streets at five for four, chickenfeed! The menace of Stryker slipped farther and farther down Sam's list of daily worries as the days and weeks and months passed and nothing happened, and that's all Stryker waited for.

That and the same attitude exhibited by his parole officer.

19—COLLECTION NIGHT

During the early days of his imprisonment, Stryker had spent hours mentally envisioning various forms of revenge and retribution directed toward Kell and Borchia.

Soon enough, he stopped this idle, juvenile day-dreaming and began actual, serious, detailed planning . . . for his revenge had two major requirements: it must be complete, absolute, resulting in total ruin; and he must not even be suspected, much less caught.

Stryker had already decided he would die before returning to prison, any prison, anywhere, any time. He could not have stood the few months he served without the great and continuous stimulation that planning revenge gave him.

His exemplary behavior after release on parole had been as much a part of his plan as the final savaging of Kell and Sam Borchia. And his behavior had another objective, finally achieved when he reported in October. The parole officer had been so impressed that he went before the judge, asked for and received a reduction of Stryker's sentence to equal that which he'd served—approximately one year including probated time. When he went for the mail two days after landing the Cessna at the ranch, Stryker had a letter from the U.S. District Court with appropriate signatures and endorsements, his final discharge from penal servitude. He was paid up; now it was his time to collect.

Stryker began making regular trips in the 180 from the ranch to a small private airport west of the city. He bought a junker car for $250 and left it at the airport. Dressed always in jeans, boots, western shirt, and wide hat, Stryker appeared to the airport personnel as just another trader; a dozen of the same breed used this airport, coming and going at all hours on their big deals, cattle in Mexico, hors-es in California, rodeos in Colorado and Texas and Arizona. Within a month Stryker became a fixture, like a bad painting on the wall—not noticed though seen regularly. The lineboys fueled the Cessna or did not, according to instructions, and made out invoices to the ranch. The one thing that aroused curiosity was that Stryker always paid cash while virtually every other aircraft owner/pilot on the field used credit cards. Within the month even this idiosyncracy became accepted routine and thus was forgotten. The airport had no control tower, only Unicom radio frequently out of order, kept no log of arrivals or departures. Though the runway was lighted at night, no personnel remained on duty between 8 p.m. and 7 a.m. Pilots needing gas, emergency repairs, transportation, etc. had access to an outside pay telephone and the airport manager's home number taped on the phone booth window.

Each flight to the city, Stryker made a dummy run, checked times, places, routes. There had been hardly any change in the routine Sam, Kell, and the girl had established, according to Bellon's report. The one slight change Stryker discovered worked to his advantage: occasionally, Kell stayed home in Sam's house alone or went out on his own. Sam kept Ethel with him almost twenty-four hours a day.

Stryker did not have to set them up; they'd done it for him.

Stryker waited for the weather. On a November afternoon wind and clouds began building from the west. His "kit" had long since been carefully thought out, readied, and packed. He dressed in long underdrawers, black jersey, new dark blue jeans. He slipped on his boots, a regular shirt, and his hat and a dark jacket. He got his kit and went out to the 180, pre-flighted, united, and took off in a gusting crosswind and outran the frontal weather system to the airport west of the city, landing just after dark. As he'd suspected, because of the weather, the airport people had closed shop and gone home. Stryker shut the 180 down, secured it, transferred his kit to his car, drove to Bella Napo-

174

li, and found Sam's car parked in its usual place. He drove on to Sam's house and saw lights inside, went on past, found a pay telephone, muffled the mouthpiece and stuck a huge chew of tobacco in his jaw, altered his voice when Kell answered.

"Sam there?"

"Naw, he's at the Bella."

"OK, thanks," Stryker said and hung up. He returned to his car and opened his kit, took off his boots, and slipped on a pair of black-dyed low-quarter tennis shoes, the soles of which he'd buffed smooth on a grindstone at the ranch. He took off his shirt, put his dark jacket back on, then slipped on a pair of black, skintight long-cuffed flying gloves. He took a Colt's .45 caliber automatic pistol from the kit and shoved it in his jacket pocket. He equipped himself with tape and a thin stainless steel bar and drove back to Sam's.

The front had arrived, with winds steady at forty and gusting to fifty, low clouds racing overhead, the smell and taste of dust in the air, and Stryker scented moisture; it would snow before morning.

He parked in front of the house but out of sight, as the house sat back almost a hundred yards from the street, along a semicircular graveled driveway. Stryker moved like a cat, all his jungle-trained combat senses attuned. He found no guards. The wind howled and slashed through thick trees, rattling limbs, rubbing them against the house. After a circuit, Stryker returned to the garage, jumped and caught the edge of the flat roof, kipped himself up and folded over at the waist so his upper body lay atop the graveled roof. He pulled his right leg up, then his left, crouched, then eased across the roof of the breezeway connecting the three-car garage and the house. Seconds later he had a windowpane taped thickly, and when a hard gust of wind hit, he rapped the glass sharply with the steel bar. The glass cracked and Stryker lifted out the shattered section, carefully worked loose the rest, then stuck his hand through and unlocked the window. A moment later he stood inside the bedroom. He went to the closed door and listened. He eased the door open and found a carpeted hallway, dimly lighted from downstairs reflection. He moved catlike and stopped at the head of the stairs, froze when Kell cursed the wind. A moment later Stryker heard the television increase volume. Stryker sat down, then inched forward, going down the stairs a step at a time on his butt, ready to duck and fire with the .45 in his fist.

The stairs went down, then turned ninety degrees. At the landing, Stryker saw Kell. The killer sat in a huge, tooled leather recliner, sipping Scotch and watching a movie. A scene ended and a commercial came on, blaring, the gain turned up to almost twice the normal volume so even if a viewer went for another drink or to the toilet he'd hear the commercial even though not seeing it. Kell swore again, then abruptly rose and Stryker lay back flat, ready, the .45 cocked. He heard ice rattle, and as the first commercial ended and a second started, Kell splashed liquor into his glass. Stryker lay and waited. The movie resumed and he heard Kell sigh.

Stryker raised up and looked. Kell again sat with his feet up, sipping. Stryker moved down the stairs, figuring the geometry of the lights so he would cast no shadow and warn Kell. He crouched and crept forward, transferred the pistol to his right hand, stood up directly behind Kell and slammed his cupped left palm across Kell's left ear with all his strength.

The concussive force shattered Kell's eardrum, and a lance of pain like pure fire went like a white-hot shaft through his head, then seemed to double back and detonate, a pain he could not believe and of such intensity he lost all control of himself, voiding his bladder and bowels as he screamed, again and again, falling forward, hugging his head in his arms, clawing at his ear, screaming.

Stryker let the hammer down on the .45 and put it in his jacket pocket. He walked around the chair, skipped lightly once, and dropkicked Kell in the guts.

Kell's eyes popped open at the kick and he stared up. His eyes bulged, a white rim showing all around the dark irises. "Oh, God, NOOOoooo. . . ."

"Oh, yes, you son of a bitch. It's collection night." Stryker let him have it again, the best left-footed punt he had straight into Kell's solar plexus. Stryker lifted the unconscious body, threw it over his shoulder, and carried Kell into the large bedroom on the ground floor. With a glance he recognized the room where Sam and the girl lived. He put Kell down on the bed, flopped him on his belly, gagged him, and tied him with strips of soft towel so no bruises would show later. Then Stryker searched. He found the safe quite easily, drawing upon his years of experience as a cop. He found the combination to the safe almost as quickly, written dimly in pencil on the bottom of a dresser drawer. He did not waste time examining the documents or counting the cash; he dumped everything into a small overnight bag from the closet—money, books, notebooks, a dozen or more tape cassettes, a locked steel box which rattled and he figured contained gems, and almost a kilo of what looked like heroin in sealed, double-layered plastic bags. Stryker frowned as he loaded the H and stepped to the bed, stripped back the sleeve of Kell's shirt. . . . No tracks. Sam? Stryker couldn't believe it. The woman? He could believe that. He began searching in the toilet and found the outfit in a blue box lined with red velvet: a blackened spoon to cook the powder down, cotton ball strainers, a throwaway plastic hypodermic needle. . . . True love!

He smiled, finding this bonus. He went back and opened one of the bags, took out a tiny pinch and prepared a dose, gave Kell a hit, hoping this wasn't pure undiluted shit, which would OD Kell. He had plans for Kell, and they did not include his death by drug overdose. In a few minutes, Kell began breathing long and deeply, easily, sighing, pleasured even in his pained unconsciousness. Stryker prepared another dose, put tape across the needle end so he could not lose the fluid, then boxed the outfit and slipped it into his pocket.

He found Kell's bedroom upstairs and discovered Sapper's equipment. Stryker recognized it at once; he'd prepared too many demolition charges, caved in too many VC bunkers, rats' nests, underground complexes, not to know plastique, blasting caps, and other materials when he saw them. He took what he needed, went downstairs and checked on Kell, then went out and drove Kell's car to the Bella Napoli. He rigged the green Cadillac. The place closed at 2 a.m., but it started snowing shortly before midnight and all the customers left by 1 a.m. When the last car departed, Stryker drove away and parked a quarter mile down the road, then went back afoot, fast.

He made himself ignore the cold and he waited. When the bodyguard-chauffeur came out, Stryker shot him through the cheek of his ass with Kell's silencer-equipped handgun. The man fell in the snow, scrabbling, shouting warning. Stryker ran, clubbed him unconscious, let the gun fall, then shot away the back door lock with the .45 and went in after Sam and the woman. He found them barricaded in Sam's office. He reloaded the .45 with a fresh clip and blasted the lock. Between shots he listened carefully. A thin smile bent his lips as he heard glass breaking, wood shattering, and the sharp, piercing sound of metal prized from the wall as Sam worked on the steel grate covering his office window.

He heard the final screech, followed by a clatter, then Sam's screeching shout, *"Get back from there, you bitch!"*

Stryker backed away from the door, shot once more, then ran at the door, dropping his shoulder and turning his head away, and crashed through. Ethel lay beneath the shattered window. Sam straddled the lower casement, half in and half out. Stryker threw a wild shot that knocked wood splinters and plaster in Sam's eyes. He shouted, *"It's collection night, Sam! I've come for your rotten ass!"*

Sam lunged and Stryker shot wide again and Sam lunged and fell out the window, hit, floundered, scrambled to his feet, and ran to his car. He jerked the door open and jumped behind the wheel and turned the key and the car blew up.

Stryker knelt beside unconscious Ethel, hiked her skirt, found where she'd been shooting dope inside her thigh, pulled the hypo out, and gave her the hit. He threw her over his shoulder and ran.

Epilogue—LOOSE ENDS DANGLING

Led by Homicide Squad commander Clyde Ruebaugh, the cops found Kell and Ethel in Sam's bed, both stoned out of their minds on dope, a syringe on the floor beside the bed. Fingernail scrapings from Kell proved to be plastique. Chemical analysis of the white powder found in the bathroom showed it to be heroin, as was the residue in the cotton ball and spoon and syringe. Upstairs Bellon and Gonzalez found Kell's equipment, more plastique, detonators, copper wire matching exactly the fragment recovered from Borchia's bombed car. The gun found beside Sam's bodyguard had Kell's fingerprints on it, as did the unfired rounds and internal parts. They lifted both Kell's and Ethel's fingerprints from the dial face and inside Sam's wall safe, the dresser drawer, on the bottom of which the cops found the safe's combination. Chino had checked Kell's car upon first arriving at Sam's house, and the engine was still hot. Sam's bodyguard admitted he'd often shot targets with Kell, using a variety of weapons, and Kell could not possibly miss Sam at that range—from door to window of Sam's office at Bella Napoli—unless he deliberately shot wide and wild. Ethel remembered nothing after the shooting started—she'd been too frightened; then Sam struck her, knocking her unconscious . . . and the next thing she knew, she woke in a room full of cops, naked, with Kell beside her, also naked. Yes, she used drugs . . . yes, she supposed she was an addict—thanks to that lousy scumbag Sam Borchia!

Kell kept saying, "No, no, no, no, no. . . ."

The trial lasted a day and a half. Kell received consecutive sentences: life for murder I and maximum penalties for conspiracy to murder, burglary of auto by explosives, attempted murder of the bodyguard, and possession of heroin with intent to sell (the intent to sell being evidenced by the amount in his possession).

Since this case was totally unrelated in any way whatever to the Stryker case, the Treasury Department secured federal grand jury indictments against Kell for possession and use of illegal firearms, interstate transportation of same, and conspiracy related to the drugs. These indictments were filed with the state prison warden and a hold placed on Kell, so in the event he ever did finish serving his hard-time with the state, he would be immediately re-arrested and taken to trial on the federal charges.

As the bailiff led Kell from the courtroom after the judge had sentenced him, Kell still muttered, "No, no, no, no, no. . . ."

Ethel tried to deal, claim immunity; but she had nothing to deal with, so she began inventing, and when finally faced with perjury as well as the original charges, she asked for a conference with the state's attorney and traded guilty pleas on all charges for minimum sentences to run concurrently. If she behaved and kept her good time, she'd be out in seven to nine years, which was tough but nothing like Kell—he had at least nine years to serve on the life sentence, without a single black mark on his record, before he could begin getting credit for the consecutive sentences on the other convictions. If he went trustie and turned stone queen for the hacks, he'd still be inside no less than twenty-five years.

Kell need not have worried, and he wasted all those long, sleepless nights awake in his cell, still muttering, "No, no, no," while he thought how unfair it all was—being in prison for the one thing he did *not* do. You were only supposed to pay for what you got caught at, not what the fuckin cops knew you'd done but couldn't prove—like Stryker's wife and kid! Stryker. He woke screaming, drenched with sweat, nightmare after nightmare, feeling once more that excruciating pain like molten steel poured into his ear . . . then the kick in the belly, and looking up, seeing *him*, eyes sunken, flesh chapped and scaly and drawn skulltight across his cheekbones, mouth like a slit, huge, deadly . . .

181

and then nothing till he woke in a room filled with cops and Ethel naked beside him. . . .

Kell need not have worried, needn't have sweated a drop over the twenty-five years' hard time staring him full face. Because Kell's conviction was a matter of extreme concern to a man in Phoenix, Arizona. The man in Phoenix was only too well aware that certain names had become internationally known. Valachi, Bonanno, Teresa, Colombo. A *ton* of books! Gambino, Accardi, Luciano, Sam The Plumber, Crazy Joe Gallo and his brothers, Meyer Lansky, Capone, Giancana hiding in Mexico. *Hiding!* Stupid bastard, every narc in the world knew where he lived in Cuernavaca, pictures of his house in the papers, him showboating around hotspots in Mexico City, Jesus *Christ!* But that wasn't *the* problem. Kell was *the* problem. That had to be taken care of. And *now* . . .!

The man in Phoenix put out the word and spread money with a lavish though secretive hand. He anticipated no problems. Within the past year a major wire service had run a major feature story on political corruption in New Mexico, stating clearly and without qualification that activities which would have caused major scandals, investigations, indictments, convictions, and jail terms other places in the U.S. were accepted as matter of course in New Mexico. The man in Phoenix felt sure he could have Kell out of the pen, either on parole or pardon or arranged escape, in a matter of weeks.

The man then began discovering that the wire service feature was highly exaggerated.

It was true that, almost as regularly as election year came around, so did a highway scandal. It was true that no police department in the entire state, including the state police, had a real civil service system; yet widespread police corruption simply did not exist.

It was true that the warden of the state penitentiary and other prison officials in New Mexico were subjected to continuous and unremitting accusations—brutality, racism, no privileges, no copies of *Playboy,* no TV, no proper rehab programs, "unrewarding" work. . . .

182

But buying a man out of that joint, the man in Phoenix discovered, could not be done.

Well, he'd tried, done his best, all he could, spent a ton of dough working for the fix; but when it's not for sale, it can't be bought, even with offers they shouldn't refuse.

So . . . Kell had to get hit in the head. A real shame. Kell was so goddam *dependable,* sixty-two hits he'd made, and never a shadow of suspicion until he collided with that Stryker bastard! But, the man had to do what had to be done. He didn't trust Kell *that* much, to do twenty-five years hard-time without cracking, without turning snitch, and Kell had worked almost exclusively for the organization for the past twenty years.

Coley Parnell's criminal record began at age 9 and he'd not gone any six consecutive months since without an arrest, except once: in 1969 he'd met Perla Portillo after a term in county jail with her brother on a theft charge. Coley fell instantly in love and so did Perla. She became pregnant and he got a job pumping gas in a Kent station and they married. The afternoon his wife gave birth, Coley's boss arrived late. Instead of waiting for his relief, Coley closed the station and caught a bus to the clinic. When he returned to the station, he'd been fired. Enraged, Coley attacked his boss with a tire iron and almost killed the man. He went inside for attempted murder. His sense of frustration, of being a perennial victim of circumstances, misunderstandings, bad breaks, and arbitrary authoritarianism increasingly drove Coley toward the edge of paranoia, and inside the joint he became incorrigible, spending more time in the hole than on the yard. By the time he'd been inside a year, he'd not only lost all his good time but had been tried and found guilty of numerous assaults upon guards and other prisoners, so he could see no daylight, no way he'd ever walk beyond those walls. The longer he stayed, the more time he owed.

The man in Phoenix was informed of Coley Parnell's circumstances through his regular intelligence sources and immediately saw the final and permanent solution to the Kell Problem.

A few days later a highly skilled, impeccably dressed, strikingly handsome young man called on Perla Portillo Parnell. Natively suspicious, living in abject poverty, even prostituting herself occasionally for rent and food money, Perla wouldn't let the man into her converted goatshed room when he first came; but he was an extremely persuasive young man. His regular trade was that of a "cooler" —the man who took over and cooled off suckers who'd been raped blind of thirty or forty grand by a crooked poker game or rigged roulette wheel. Perla only knew him as Johnny, and his name did not matter. Johnny gave her a bank deposit slip and a checkbook.

The following day Perla left her baby with a neighbor and caught a bus downtown, and verified she now had $10,000. She bought clothes, rented a decent apartment, found a nursery for the child, filled her cupboards with food, and with her improved appearance and assured safety for the baby, she got a job.

When she went to Santa Fe two weeks later for her monthly visit with Coley, he asked if she'd gotten any money. She told him what had happened. He nodded and said, "OK, now forget me. Forget me! I gotta do a job," and left her bewildered in the visiting room.

In the morning paper two days later she learned that Coley had murdered another prisoner, a man named Kell . . . and she had just as well forget Coley. He was killed after murdering Kell and knifing a hack.

The man in Phoenix counted this a double bonus and sighed hugely with relief. In fact, he felt so well he summoned his personal bodyguard and told him to make arrangements for some fishing, and an hour later he sat back totally relaxed in his special vibrator chair, drink in hand, as his private jet lifted off the runway and turned toward Mexico. Johnny, the exceptionally persuasive, handsome young man who'd made the deal with Perla Parnell, sat across the aisle, talking softly, his hand up the dress of a girl known nationwide for her toothpaste commercials. The older man smiled, hoping the lad enjoyed himself. Johnny would not make the return trip. The man from Phoenix sighed again, smoothed back the thick gray hair above his ears, took another sip of his drink, content beyond measure with the knowledge that everything had been taken care of . . . or soon would be. He looked at the young man again, and sighed.

The contented man would not have been so relaxed had he known that the moment he took the last sip and emptied his glass, Colin Stryker sat in Perla Portillo Parnell's apartment and waited patiently for her to come home from work. . . .

For the circumstances of Coley's attack upon Kell, his suicidal eagerness to die, Perla's sudden affluence, and the tape of their last conversation monitored in the penitentiary's visiting room—from all those summed together Stryker knew:

The debt hadn't been paid in full, not yet. Collecting in full went beyond the Sapper and Ethel and stupid Sam, a long, long way past them.

Bestsellers by
William Crawford

THE CHINESE CONNECTION, by William Crawford. A novel of violence and suspense on the Mexican border. This is an absorbing tale of drug running and murder in the Southwest—with strange ties to the Far East. With a unique and richly conceived cast of characters, it reveals a world of which *The French Connection* offered a first hint. For these are people who would stop at nothing to attain their goals—for whom violence, sex, bribery and assassination are only way stations on the road to the big money, and to the power that money will buy. It's up to one honest man—a man not afraid to kill—to stop the scheme.
P00232-6—95¢

THE MARINE, by William Crawford. A stirring novel of war, heroism, patriotism. It's Jim Garrison's story—a U.S. Marine and 100% American. However, this isn't a story of handsome men in fancy dress uniforms, or the spectacle of military parades . . . it's a gut-rending, realistic account of a man trying to survive a war. And he does make it, through the hell of it all—brutality, starvation, torture. Then Jim is hit with an even more grisly situation. He has to face trial for his action in a Vietnam POW camp! His court martial puts his life on the line, and we find that the trial is also a test of our military traditions and patriotism.
P00126-6—95¢

GUNSHIP COMMANDER. A fast-moving story of the helicopter war in Vietnam. This is the heroic story of one man—a man alone in a strange and savage war. Joe Brown, an Indian, wanted to live so he had to fight. He'd already been on four tours of duty as a helicopter pilot in Vietnam and he'd had his fill of suffering to survive. But he went back to the 504th—a group riddled by race, drug, moral and discipline problems. It was bad—fighting his fellow officers, and others, who didn't like the war anymore than he did.
P00255-6—95¢

This is your Order Form . . .
Just clip and mail.

TO ORDER
Please check the space next to the book/s you want, send this order form together with your check or money order, include the price of the book/s and 15¢ for handling and mailing, to:
PINNACLE BOOKS, INC.
P.O. Box 4347 Grand Central Station/New York, N. Y. 10017

_____ P00126-6	THE MARINE	95¢
_____ P00232-6	THE CHINESE CONNECTION	95¢
_____ P00255-6	GUNSHIP COMMANDER	95¢

☐ CHECK HERE IF YOU WANT A FREE CATALOGUE.

I have enclosed $_____ check_____ or money order_____ as payment in full. No C.O.D.'s.

Name_____

Address_____

City_____ State_____ Zip_____
(Please allow time for delivery.)

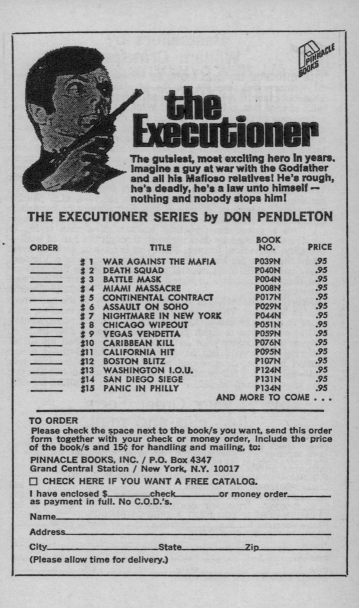

the Executioner

The gutsiest, most exciting hero in years. Imagine a guy at war with the Godfather and all his Mafioso relatives! He's rough, he's deadly, he's a law unto himself — nothing and nobody stops him!

THE EXECUTIONER SERIES by DON PENDLETON

ORDER		TITLE	BOOK NO.	PRICE
_____	# 1	WAR AGAINST THE MAFIA	P039N	.95
_____	# 2	DEATH SQUAD	P040N	.95
_____	# 3	BATTLE MASK	P004N	.95
_____	# 4	MIAMI MASSACRE	P008N	.95
_____	# 5	CONTINENTAL CONTRACT	P017N	.95
_____	# 6	ASSAULT ON SOHO	P029N	.95
_____	# 7	NIGHTMARE IN NEW YORK	P044N	.95
_____	# 8	CHICAGO WIPEOUT	P051N	.95
_____	# 9	VEGAS VENDETTA	P059N	.95
_____	#10	CARIBBEAN KILL	P076N	.95
_____	#11	CALIFORNIA HIT	P095N	.95
_____	#12	BOSTON BLITZ	P107N	.95
_____	#13	WASHINGTON I.O.U.	P124N	.95
_____	#14	SAN DIEGO SIEGE	P131N	.95
_____	#15	PANIC IN PHILLY	P134N	.95

AND MORE TO COME . . .

TO ORDER
Please check the space next to the book/s you want, send this order form together with your check or money order. Include the price of the book/s and 15¢ for handling and mailing, to:

PINNACLE BOOKS, INC. / P.O. Box 4347
Grand Central Station / New York, N.Y. 10017

☐ CHECK HERE IF YOU WANT A FREE CATALOG.

I have enclosed $_____ check _____ or money order _____
as payment in full. No C.O.D.'s.

Name_____

Address_____

City_____ State_____ Zip_____

(Please allow time for delivery.)

PINNACLE BOOKS

ALL NEW DYNAMITE SERIES

THE DESTROYER

by Richard Sapir & Warren Murphy

CURE, the world's most secret crime-fighting organization created the perfect weapon — Remo Williams — man programmed to become a cold, calculating death machine. The super man of the 70's!

Order		Title	Book No.	Price
	# 1	Created, The Destroyer	P038N	95¢
	# 2	Death Check	P072N	95¢
	# 3	Chinese Puzzle	P078N	95¢
	# 4	Mafia Fix	P104N	95¢
	# 5	Dr. Quake	P125N	95¢
	# 6	Death Therapy	P136N	95¢
	# 7	Union Bust	P149N	95¢
	# 8	Summit Chase	P165N	95¢
	# 9	Murder's Shield	P179N	95¢
	#10	Terror Squad	P196N	95¢
	#11	Kill or Cure	P230N	95¢
	#12	Slave Safari	P258N	95¢
			and more to come . . .	

TO ORDER
Please check the space next to the book/s you want, send this order form together with your check or money order, include the price of the book/s and 15¢ for handling and mailing, to:
PINNACLE BOOKS, INC. / P.O. Box 4347
Grand Central Station / New York, N.Y. 10017
☐ **CHECK HERE IF YOU WANT A FREE CATALOG.**
I have enclosed $_____ check_____ or money order_____ as payment in full. No C.O.D.'s.

Name_____

Address_____

City_____ State_____ Zip_____
(Please allow time for delivery.)

PINNACLE BOOKS

THE "BUTCHER,"
the only man to leave
the Mafia—and live!
A man forever on the run,
unable to trust anyone,
condemned to a life
of constant violence!

THE BUTCHER SERIES

by Stuart Jason

Order		Title	Book No.	Price
_____	#1	KILL QUICK OR DIE	P011	95¢
_____	#2	COME WATCH HIM DIE	P025	95¢
_____	#3	KEEPERS OF DEATH	P084	95¢
_____	#4	BLOOD DEBT	P111	95¢
_____	#5	DEADLY DEAL	P152	95¢
_____	#6	KILL TIME	P197	95¢
_____	#7	DEATH RACE	P228	95¢
_____	#8	FIRE BOMB	P272	95¢
_____	#9	SEALED WITH BLOOD	P279	95¢

and more to come . . .

TO ORDER
Please check the space next to the book/s you want, send this order
form together with your check or money order, include the price of
the book/s and 15¢ for handling and mailing, to:

PINNACLE BOOKS, INC. / P.O. Box 4347
Grand Central Station / New York, N. Y. 10017

☐ Check here if you want a free catalog.

I have enclosed $_____ check_____ or money order_____
as payment in full. No C.O.D.'s.

Name_____

Address_____

City_____ State_____ Zip_____
(Please allow time for delivery.)